Joanne Rock credits her decision to write romance to when a book she picked up during a flight delay engrossed her so thoroughly that she didn't mind at all when her flight was delayed two more times. Giving her readers the chance to escape into another world has motivated her to write over eighty books for a variety of Mills & Boon series.

Rancher
in Her Bed
JOANNE ROCK

MILLS & BOON

First published in Great Britain 2019
by Mills & Boon, an imprint of HarperCollins*Publishers*
1 London Bridge Street, London, SE1 9GF

Large Print edition 2019

© 2019 Harlequin Books S.A.

Special thanks and acknowledgement are given
to Joanne Rock for her contribution to the
Texas Cattleman's Club: Houston miniseries.

ISBN: 978-0-263-08367-5

Printed and bound in Great Britain
by CPI Group (UK) Ltd, Croydon, CR0 4YY

One

Frankie Walsh understood that her generation had killed romance.

Sure, some people said that dating apps were responsible. And it was true the swipe-left mentality definitely smothered every last hope of spontaneity and excitement. But whether the blame rested with millennials or apps or the parenting that had let a crop of kids grow up thinking they were the center of the universe, Frankie agreed with the consensus among her girlfriends that romance was a thing of the past.

Which begged the question, why was she lingering outside the main house at Currin Ranch, heart fluttering wildly while she hoped for a sighting of her boss, Xander Currin?

Because she was ten kinds of foolish, that's why. She'd already accomplished her errand here—a two-second task of retrieving the keys to the barn where the haying equipment was stored. Xander had kindly left them outside the back entrance on a huge wooden patio table, right where the maintenance manager had told her they'd be. One of the other hands who'd helped with the haying equipment yesterday was out sick today, and he'd accidentally taken the other set.

Frankie had volunteered for the errand so fast the other ranch hands had all looked at her sideways. If she wasn't careful, her ill-advised crush on Xander would become a running joke all over Currin Ranch. She valued this job too much to make her workplace uncomfortable that way, and she'd strived for too long to prove she could hold her own with the physical demands of the job.

With the fear of being laughed at spurring her boots, she jammed the keys into the back pocket of her jeans and turned away from the massive log mansion overlooking a creek bed. She kept to the stone path that wound past the pool house and through a low shrubbery hedge, returning to the edge of the lawn where she'd left the energetic young mare, Carmen, she'd ridden over. Her time spent with the animals was the best reward of the job and a necessary part of the requirements for veterinary school. If she could ever make enough money to pay for it.

Yet another reason why this job was so crucial for her. Her other gigs were of the volunteer variety—shadowing a local vet on his calls during her off days and helping out at a local animal shelter. Currin Ranch was the only job she had that came with a paycheck.

Stroking the mare's flank, she was just

about to mount up when she heard laughter and voices in the backyard. Male. And female.

A warning prickled along the back of her neck, urging her to go. Or maybe calling her to stay? Because she recognized the deep tone of the man, a warm and sexy chuckle pitched low in a way that made Frankie's skin heat. The object of her silly crush.

But a fluffy feminine giggle smothered any wayward thoughts Frankie might have been entertaining about Xander. Frozen in place, she watched as the couple emerged from the shrubbery together. Xander escorted a strawberry blonde in a bright yellow sundress that accentuated considerable curves. The woman's glossy waves bounced along with everything else as she tapped her way down the path in kitten heels. Reaching the driveway less than ten yards from where Frankie stood, the woman didn't so much as glance her way as she lifted a hand to wave goodbye to Xander. She slid into an ice-blue convertible that looked like it cost more than veterinary school.

Had she been an overnight guest?

Jealousy flared. Feeling every inch the ranch hand she was, Frankie fought an urge to at least swipe a dusty streak off the front of her jeans. Instead, she hauled herself up on the mare's back even as the horse startled sideways away from the convertible's racing engine.

It was all Frankie could do not to glare at the woman for punching the accelerator while the vehicle was still in Park. Blondie squealed the tires on her way out.

Soothing the mare with a reassuring hold on the reins and a squeeze against her flanks, Frankie was about to turn tail and ride for the barn when she noticed Xander charging her way. Tall and muscular, he wore his jeans and fitted tee with the ease of any other ranch foreman, but as the heir to the Currin family fortune, there was something commanding about his presence. Right now, with his blue eyes fixed on the horse and his stubble-shadowed dark jaw flexing, he had an air of restrained danger. The allure of a man who could hold his own with a surly beast without breaking a sweat.

"Whoa. Easy, Carmen," he called to the anxious palomino, his stance the same one the ranch trainer used when breaking a new mount, positioned just outside the reach of her dancing forefeet. "Easy."

"She's okay," Frankie assured him, leaning back slightly in the saddle to cue the mare. "I've got her."

Her heart sped faster, more from her boss's sudden appearance at her side than the mild scare with Carmen. Frankie wouldn't have taken her if she'd felt the least bit uneasy with the spirited youngster. Besides, keeping her seat on Carmen was a cakewalk compared to bronc riding, the rodeo event Frankie had recently taken up. She'd tried it on a dare from one of the other ranch hands and discovered she wasn't too bad at it. And considering how badly she could use the extra money, she couldn't deny the appeal of the cash prizes.

Xander peered up at her with narrowed eyes.

"I didn't think the trainer had cleared this one for work." Shifting closer, his gaze darted from the horse to her and back again. "Carmen hasn't been with us long."

Her boss reached to stroke the palomino's muzzle, his dark hair a stark contrast to the horse's golden coat and white mane. She was used to seeing him in his black Stetson around the ranch in his work as the foreman.

Much to his father's frustration.

Everyone involved with Currin Ranch knew that Ryder Currin wanted his only son in the family's oil business and not overseeing the ranching operation. But for the eleven months that Frankie had been on staff, Xander had been personally involved with everything from the herd to the haying, making sure the collective efforts ran smoothly. He was good at his job, but even she knew the foreman's role wasn't where the heir apparent belonged.

"I'm not using her for work today," she explained, forcing herself to relax, if only for Carmen's sake. She hadn't meant to rile the boss. "I rode her over to pick up the barn key because she seemed restless. I thought she could use an outing."

Why couldn't Xander's blue eyes be focused on her for positive reasons and not because he thought she'd screwed up? So many times, she'd hoped to snag his attention, and now, when she'd finally accomplished it, he seemed on edge. Irritated, even.

"Not cleared for work means no riding." His jaw flexed as he moved closer, stroking down Carmen's neck to her shoulder, quieting the animal. By now, his shoulder neared Frankie's calf, his body in tantalizing proximity. "A good ranch horse doesn't spook at engine noises. No sense putting her in a position to fail when she isn't ready yet."

Frankie bit down on the inside of her lip to keep from pointing out that an over-revved

Italian luxury car wasn't the kind of "engine noise" horses heard in the normal course of ranch work. Neither was screechy bubble-gum pop dialed up to full blast on a convertible stereo as his guest peeled out of the driveway.

Then again, she didn't think she could muster an impartial "yes sir" when he was dead wrong about Carmen. Carefully, she quit gnawing on the inside of her lip so she could speak.

"Then I guess I'd better get her back to the barn." Frankie managed a tight smile. "I'll let the trainer know Carmen needs to broaden her musical tolerance."

Xander's head snapped up to look at her, his dark brows angling down with his frown.

Had that slipped out?

Her fake smile froze in place.

In the silent moment that followed, she became aware of the soft buzz of electric hedge trimmers as a gardener worked nearby. The scent of cut grass hung in the Texas June air, growing more sweltering with each breath.

"What's your name again?" he asked, a warning note in his voice.

Was he going to write her up? He couldn't fire her for being a smart-ass, could he? She really needed this job and the hundred hours of animal care that would help her get an interview for vet school. She might have been on staff for almost a year, but she'd only just started working more directly with the horses.

For the first six months she'd done only the worst of the grunt work, no doubt why the boss hadn't recalled her name.

"Frankie Walsh," she said quickly, kicking herself for spouting off and tugging her hat just a little lower on her forehead. Wishing she could hide. "Thanks for the key."

He gave her a nod but didn't step back, a barrier of impressive muscle and denim. "The rules are in place for a reason. Not just to keep Carmen safe, but the ranch staff, as well."

That caught her off guard.

"Meaning me?" She shook her head, her

ponytail swiping across her back as she thought about all the times she'd landed on her butt in local rodeo competitions. Bronc riding wasn't for the faint of heart. "No need to worry about my safety. I'm tougher than I look."

Turning to go, she hoped Xander would forget about the embarrassing encounter.

Her ego was the only thing bruised, after all. His safety concerns were misplaced. Clearly, he favored a softer kind of woman than Frankie would ever be, which was just as well since she should be concentrating on earning enough money to live her dreams instead of mooning over her off-limits boss. There was an open rodeo at a local county fair next weekend, and she needed to be focused if she was going to enter the saddle bronc competition, a sport attracting more women in recent years. She could ride better than most of the other hands at Currin Ranch, and it wasn't like the small rodeo would attract many female competitors.

She hoped.

She had an outside chance of walking away with the prize—enough money to buy herself a coveted ticket to the Texas Cattleman's Club Flood Relief Gala. The swanky event would be a great place to see the other side of the ranching world and meet the wealthy ranch owners she hoped to one day serve with her veterinary practice.

Better to scuttle back to the barns and forget about Xander. Romance was dead anyhow, right?

Even so, she could almost feel the foreman's gaze following her as she rode away. And she'd be lying if she said it didn't give her a Texas-sized thrill.

A battle of the bands was in full progress when Xander parked his truck outside the fairgrounds for a Friday night rodeo. Because Currin Ranch was a major sponsor of the event, he'd been allowed to park right near the barbecue cook-off pavilion where he was meeting his father for their weekly dinner together.

Normally, dinner with Ryder Currin was a long, drawn-out affair since his father appreciated five-star dining, an attentive waitstaff and the best vintages a wine cellar had to offer. But since Xander would take barbecue from a Texas grill master over a four-course meal any day of the week, tonight's supper promised to be a whole lot more fun.

Besides, a shorter dinner meant less time for his dad to quiz him about when he was going to return to the front office of the family's oil business.

Dropping his Stetson on his head, he stepped out of the pickup and into the hubbub of a rodeo night. Boots crunching on dry gravel, he walked through the VIP gate as the growing crowd broke into enthusiastic applause for the country band sweating under the gazebo's canopy of decorative lights. The sawdust-covered dance floor was almost full even though it was early. The rodeo wouldn't start for another hour, and the carnival rides were in full swing despite the heat. The scent of slow-roasted brisket hung heavy in the air, grills smoking around the perimeter of the pavilion where chefs from all over the state prepped their best ribs and pulled pork.

"Xander," a familiar deep voice called from inside the covered dining area. "Over here."

Spotting his dad, he edged past a family maneuvering a stroller through the crowd, then joined Ryder at one of the few private tables in the reserved section up front.

His father never wore a suit but somehow, even in jeans and a button-down shirt, he still carried himself with considerable authority. With his boots and his dark brown Stetson, Ryder wore much the same outfit as the rest of the rodeo-goers, yet looked like a man in charge.

"Hope you don't mind, but I took the liberty of ordering a little of everything." Ryder leaned back in his chair as a curvy redhead in a fringed shirt and denim miniskirt delivered a tray full of barbecue steaming from at least ten different plates. Two beer bottles reigned over the center of the tray.

While the server set out a basket of biscuits, the beers and food, Xander steeled himself for the weekly interrogation about his life, his career plans and how soon he'd be ready to give up his "wild hair" of working the land. The dinners were Ryder's thinly veiled way of delivering regular guilt trips about not fulfilling his family obligations.

Xander might still live in a private wing of his father's home, but they rarely saw each other around the ranch. Ryder Currin kept his personal affairs closely guarded. Rumors had been flying around the Texas Cattleman's Club recently that Ryder was seeing Angela Perry, the daughter of his bitter business rival, Sterling. But Xander wasn't about to ask his dad about that.

"I happen to know she's single," Ryder observed as the server walked away from their table. He tipped his head in the departing woman's direction. "In case you're interested."

Xander's thoughts were so far from women it took him a moment to realize what his dad was talking about. Strangely, the only female who'd been circling his thoughts lately was a fierce brunette named Frankie, of all people.

The willowy ranch hand with the big green eyes and dust-smeared jeans wasn't Xander's type, but something about her prickly attitude and challenging stare had gotten under his skin.

"Definitely not interested," he told his father honestly, taking his hat off and settling it on the empty chair beside him. "And I'm pretty sure I passed the stage where I needed your help closing the deal with a woman at least a decade ago."

He plucked one of the longnecks from the center of the table and took a sip.

Ryder chuckled. "I suppose that's fair. Are you still dating Kenzie then?" he pressed, lifting his own beer for a swig. "I thought I saw her car parked outside the house last week."

A loudspeaker announcement called the

contestants for the mutton-busting event into the arena, and a handful of families with kids hurried out of the dining pavilion. The band kept playing, their amps only muted periodically for the PA system. Behind them, the big Ferris wheel turned slowly, the neon lights flashing on the spokes even though it wasn't dark out yet.

"No. She only dropped in that morning to ask me to judge the rodeo queen competition with her." Xander had escorted her back to her car as fast as possible, knowing she'd only inquired about the rodeo queen pageant as an excuse to stop by. To see why he hadn't called. "But I'm not ready for a relationship with her or anyone else. Not after—"

The stab of pain over losing his fiancée in a tragic horse fall had eased in the last two years, but he felt as certain as ever that he wouldn't tread down that path to love and happily-ever-after again. That relationship had been complicated, with unhappy layers he hadn't ever understood. And in the end, it had gutted him. So working the land had

been the only thing that offered any healing, and Xander wasn't willing to give that
up anytime soon.

"I understand." Leaning forward in his
chair, Ryder turned serious. "Better than you
think. When I lost Elinah—" His lips compressed into a flat line at the mention of his
second wife, who'd died of cancer thirteen
years ago. "I know it's not easy to love again
after losing someone."

Xander had only been twelve at the time,
and he hadn't been living with his father
then, spending most of his time with his
mother, Penny, Ryder's first wife. But even
as a kid, Xander had seen how his father retreated into himself for years afterward. Elinah had been the love of his life.

Now he appreciated his father's understanding.

"To be honest, I've got zero interest in
the whole idea of love." Drawing one of the
plates of ribs closer, he took a big bite.

"No need to rule it out altogether," his father cautioned, ignoring his vibrating phone

next to him on the table. "Maybe you'll meet someone at the Texas Cattleman's Club Flood Relief Gala tomorrow night." He gave Xander a level stare. "You *are* attending, I trust?"

Ryder had already insisted on it, since he was hosting the event himself. Xander had no desire to spend the evening at a black-tie shindig, but he planned to support his father in his ongoing war with Sterling Perry for control of the Houston branch of the Texas Cattleman's Club.

While Sterling might be a wealthy businessman with a vast company that dealt in real estate, construction and property management, Xander didn't trust the guy. Part of that was because Sterling hated and resented Xander's father, of course. But Xander found it tough to respect a ranch owner who never spent any time on the land, and that was Sterling to a T. He might own the prosperous Perry Ranch, but that didn't mean its success had anything to do with his ranching IQ.

"I'm going stag." Xander had a spare

ticket, but his awkward meeting with Kenzie had reinforced his decision to engage in only the most superficial kinds of affairs. She'd clearly been upset with him when she'd squealed her tires on her way out of the driveway.

If Frankie Walsh hadn't been such an accomplished horsewoman, Kenzie's childish act could have seriously endangered the ranch hand. Frankie had really handled herself well, especially on an excitable young mare.

"There will be plenty of single women there, anyway." His father wiped his hands on a paper napkin as their server appeared to clear a few of the plates. He waited until she retreated to finish his thought. "Just keep an open mind where romance is concerned."

Not going to happen, Dad. But as soon as he thought that, Frankie's long legs and sexy smile smoked through his thoughts. He willed away her image and took another swig of his beer. The sound of cowbells and cheering erupted from the nearby arena, and he guessed the children's rodeo event had started, a precursor to the adult competitions that would start soon.

"Most of the women I meet are more interested in the Currin name. Or the fortune. Or—" he'd been about to say *my sexual prowess*, but that hardly seemed like a topic to share "—who knows what. But regardless, I'll be there tomorrow."

Another announcement came over the loudspeaker for the barrel-racing contestants. Showtime must be soon. Xander gladly used it as an excuse to finish his meal.

"I'd better get into the arena." He'd asked his father to meet him here for their weekly meal since several employees were competing in tonight's events. "I want to wish the guys good luck before things get under way."

And yes, a part of him wondered if he'd see Frankie. She might attend to support the other hands. Or hell, maybe she'd be competing in the barrel race or one of the other women's events. He really didn't know much about her, which was unlike him.

Truth was, he'd avoided her the few times their paths had come close to crossing around Currin Ranch. He'd felt the pull toward her before and had always tamped it down deep, unwilling to get drawn into that kind of affair with someone who worked for him. He only knew she had the least seniority around the ranch up until a few months ago, when they'd brought on a new kid, which meant Frankie often got stuck with some of the worst jobs.

"Sure." Ryder lifted his beer. "If I don't see you inside, I'll definitely catch up with you at the gala, son."

Nodding, Xander scooped up his hat and replaced it on his head before leaving the dining pavilion.

Outside the arena, he could see the flag bearer lining up on horseback with her attendants. A few rodeo clowns waited with them, part of the processional that would kick things off soon. Inside the open arena with its high metal roof and dirt floor, Xander could see a couple of kids in cowboy hats riding the sheep used for the mutton-busting competition. The crowd was cheering, cow-bells rang and the event announcer narrated the action.

He'd been to plenty of rodeos, from the big Houston Livestock Show to the local Friday night events like this one, and he enjoyed the small-town, grassroots competitions far more. While he appreciated the national spotlight that the multibillion-dollar rodeo industry brought to ranching, he had more fun at the community affairs that celebrated the hardworking men and women who made their living off the land.

Ranching was tough, but there was some-thing cathartic about putting in the hard manual labor day after day and seeing the results firsthand.

"Hey, boss!" someone shouted from be-hind the chutes.

Peering over that way, Xander spotted a throng of soon-to-be competitors congre-gating, black-and-white numbers pinned to their Western shirts. A bowlegged cowboy was flagging him down, waving the end of his lasso.

Xander recognized Reggie Malloy, a long-time member of the Currin Ranch team. He headed that way, sidestepping a few families retrieving their kids after the mutton-busting event.

"Good to see you, Reggie." He clapped the senior-most herdsman on the shoulder. "Just came down to wish everyone well before the competitions start."

They moved out of the way of the stock contractors bringing in the calves for the first round of roping events. Out in the arena, the procession to kick off the rodeo began. Purple spotlights circled the venue, casting streaks across Reggie's face as they spoke.

"We're all fired up down here," Reggie told him with a wide grin, his cheeks red from the heat. He wore a championship buckle that broadcast his experience in roping. "My money's on the new kid, Wyatt, to do the ranch proud tonight. I've been working with him off and on since Christmas, and he's come a long way."

"That's good of you, Reg. The young guys all look up to you." He lowered his voice as the crowd quieted for the national anthem.

Even the people backstage went still. Only the calves shuffled their feet while a local high school girl dressed in red, white and blue belted out the song. When she finished, the crowd cheered and the announcer started to rev things up.

Reggie tucked his rope under one arm and started to head back toward the other competitors in the first go-round. "Boss, you might want to stick around for the lady bronc riders later."

"Lady bronc riders?" He'd been to plenty of rodeos before, and it wasn't often that he'd seen women competing in rough stock events, especially at the smaller venues like this one.

"There are more and more of them," Reggie assured him while the rodeo clowns performed a few tricks to warm up the crowd.

"There are only a few signed up tonight, but our own Frankie Walsh is one of them. I've seen her ride and she's not bad."

Frankie?

A vision of the ranch hand on the back of a bucking bronc flashed through his mind. Followed by memories of Rena's fall. He hadn't been there the day his fiancée had been thrown, but that had never stopped his brain from imagining it thousands of times.

His gut balled up in a cold knot.

"Where is she?" Clammy sweat popped out along his brow. "Where's Frankie?"

He needed to talk her out of it. No, he needed to lay down the law and tell her she couldn't compete. What in the hell was she thinking to tempt fate like that? Bronc riding was a dangerous sport for anyone—man or woman.

"You okay?" Reggie's blond brows knit. Frowning, the wrangler reached for a bottled water resting on an empty bleacher off to one side. "Have a drink. You don't look so good."

Swiping a hand along his forehead, he tried to shut off the images flashing through his mind.

"I'm fine. Just—" He was already scouring the arena for any sign of the saucy brunette with killer legs. "Where's Frankie?"

Reggie pointed outside the arena. "Last I saw her, she was heading outside to give herself a pep talk. Looked to me like she was walking in the direction of the Ferris wheel."

Xander's boots were already in motion.

Two

Frankie paced quick circles around a broken passenger cart tucked behind the Ferris wheel, out of the way of the kids and couples in line for their turn on the carnival attraction.

Nerves always set in before an event like this. She'd only done half a dozen rodeos, but she recognized the mixture of butterflies and doubt that came before the exhilaration of her moment in the arena. This part—the waiting—was far more of a challenge than the eight seconds she needed to last on the back of a bucking horse.

Rock music blared from the ride's sound system, competing with a local country band playing nearby, the pings and whistles of various skills competitions along the carnival main strip, and the shouts of carnies urging on the guests to play longer. Spend more. Every now and then, an announcement over the loudspeaker reminded the fair attendees who needed to report to the arena next for their event in the rodeo. Barrel racers, calf ropers and wranglers of all sorts took their turn.

Pacing faster as she let herself get keyed up, Frankie knew tonight would be tough. There were only a handful of lady competitors in the saddle bronc event. But she'd seen the list and recognized the names of two top-notch riders from an all-women's tour that had made its way around Texas the year before. She'd seen those ladies live and guessed she didn't have much of a shot against them tonight.

Then again…who knew?

The broncs could surprise anyone. And

Frankie had never walked away from a challenge. Her mother had told her more than once it was her worst failing.

Not that she was going to think about her adoptive mom. Or dad. Or the home she'd run from the moment she'd turned eighteen. She'd save those worries for another night, when she wasn't about to risk her neck.

"Frankie."

A man's voice cut clean through her tumultuous thoughts. Her head snapped up to see Xander Currin striding toward her.

Purposefully.

A thrill shot through her at the sight of him in his dark jeans and a fitted black button-down. His Stetson was the same one he usually wore, but his boots were an upgrade from the ones he wore for work. His blue eyes zeroed in on her face, stirring more butterflies.

"Yes?" Puzzled that he would seek her out, she listened hard to hear over her galloping heartbeat.

He didn't look pleased. He couldn't possibly still be mad about her taking Carmen out the other day, could he?

"I just saw Reggie." Her boss stopped a few feet away from her, closer than he'd ever stood before. "He told me you're entering the saddle bronc event."

"That's right." Relief seeped through the awareness of him. He wasn't here to give her a hard time about riding Carmen. "There's a ladies' competition tonight."

"Do you have any idea how dangerous rough stock events can be?" His voice was all sharp edges and accusation, just like the last time they'd spoken.

Defensiveness flared. How was it she could irritate this man just by existing?

"I work with horses and cattle every day, the same as you do. I suppose I know a thing or two about them." She folded her arms, refusing to let him intimidate her here, off the Currin Ranch.

She'd worked too hard in life to be steam-rollered by people who thought they knew what was best for her.

"That doesn't mean you're ready to ride a surly, pissed-off beast trained to buck." His jaw clenched. "Do you know how hard riders prepare for this event?"

A burst of applause broke out at a nearby midway game while she reeled from Xander's sexist audacity.

"Did you give Reggie the same speech you're giving me?" She felt a flash of impatience that bordered on anger. "Or Wyatt, the greenest of your employees entering a competition tonight?"

Xander's lips flattened into a thin line. "No. But—"

"Then don't you think you're being a chauvinist to call me out for doing an event that I have spent time preparing for and that I'm actually good at?"

His expression shifted slightly, some of the tension around his eyes easing a fraction. He seemed to force in a deep breath before responding.

"You have a reputation as a very hard worker around the ranch, but if you've been training for this, it's the first I've heard," he acknowledged, dialing back the confrontational tone.

And taking a bit of the wind from her sails along with it.

"Well, I don't have much spare time to train given my schedule." Some days she ached so much from the physical grind of the labor she did, she could barely force her arms to shovel food in her mouth before showering and heading to bed. "I take as many hours as I can to make ends meet."

She lifted her chin, daring him to find fault in that. There was no shame in hard work.

The country band playing nearby launched into a crowd-pleasing favorite, eliciting whistles and shouts from the dancers on the other side of the Ferris wheel. Neon lights blinked in varying shades as the spokes of the ride spun past them.

"I don't want you in that arena tonight," Xander informed her, his eyes utterly serious.

She reminded herself she worked for him.

That she didn't want to land on the wrong side of the powerful Currin family. But damn it, who did he think he was to call the shots for her tonight?

"That's too bad," she found herself saying anyhow, "because I'm not on the clock now, which means you can't order me around."

Xander glanced away from her and then back again. More gently, he asked, "Can you tell me why it's so important to you to enter an event so fundamentally dangerous?"

Something in his voice compelled her. So she decided to be honest.

"I'm working hard all the time trying to earn enough money to put myself through veterinary school, and I don't get many breaks." She forced herself to unclasp her folded arms. To stand up straighter and own her thoughts and feelings. "And when I heard about the Texas Cattleman's Club Flood Relief Gala, I thought *that* was the kind of break I'd love—something fun and different that would let me have a glimpse of the life I'm working toward. A chance to see the reward with my own eyes to keep me on the path. You know?"

Xander cocked his head like he didn't quite understand.

"You want to go to the Flood Relief Gala," he said slowly.

"I do. It's healthy to give yourself some tangible rewards in the process of working toward a big goal," she explained, sharing an insight gleaned from a college counselor who'd helped her figure out how to start on a path toward achieving her big dreams. "And the prize money tonight will give me enough to afford a ticket to the gala."

The loudspeaker blared a call for the competitors in her event. Nerves fluttered in her stomach.

Because of the upcoming ride or the man?

"I've got to go." She took a step forward, but he stepped in front of her.

"You can't enter, Frankie. I mean it."

How had she missed all the signs that her boss was this bullheaded? "You can't fire me for being in the rodeo when you've got five other employees entering."

Eyes on the arena, she didn't want to lose her spot. She started forward again.

"Then I'll make you a deal," Xander offered, his voice deep. "If you don't set foot in that arena tonight, I'll take you to the gala as my guest."

She stopped. Turned back to look at him. Gauged his expression.

"Since you can't fire me, you'll take me to the gala as your…guest?" She found that hard to believe. Xander Currin could have his pick of beautiful, accomplished women. "Why would you do that?"

Her heartbeat sped in a way that didn't have a damned thing to do with nerves or the competition about to begin. Her racing pulse had everything to do with Xander's blue eyes on her. And the potential of what he offered.

"You said you wanted a ticket. I'm offering you one." He sidestepped her question neatly. "Be my date tomorrow night."

"What's in it for you?" She knew better than to think her boss wanted to date her.

"I've got two tickets." He spoke clearly enough, but sure didn't explain. "Would you like one or not?"

She couldn't argue. Not when she knew her chance of nabbing that prize money was small with the level of competition here. Furthermore, how many times had she indulged fantasies about this man? An evening with him would be...exciting. To say the least.

"Very well." She swallowed back the surge of feminine awareness. She couldn't believe she was going to be her boss's date at such a huge, important event. "I will go to the gala with you."

"Good." He didn't look happy so much as relieved. "Now let's get out of here. I'll take you back to the ranch."

Disappointment stung a bit, but she told herself to be happy for the unexpected opportunity she'd just won.

"You don't want to see how the guys do tonight?" she asked, hating to leave and not support the rest of the ranch team. The guys at Currin Ranch were her only family now.

Living on-site at the ranch made the group close-knit.

"I'm not taking any chances you'll change your mind." Xander palmed her back, briefly, steering her toward the exit. "My truck is right through this gate."

The one marked VIP. Of course.

His touch stirred her senses. She tried to hold on to her frustration with him, but it was tougher to do with the memory of that brief caress between her shoulder blades still warming her through her shirt.

"You don't have to take me home. I can catch a ride with the guys." She didn't want them to worry about her. "Reggie will wonder what happened to me—"

"I'll text him." He withdrew a phone while they walked out of the fairgrounds into the parking area. He made a few taps on the screen and then shoved it back in his pocket. "There. Done."

She wondered what it must be like to be a

Currin and have the world ordered to your personal preference at all times. She'd fallen right in line, too, unable to argue with someone who could fulfill her wish for a ticket as easily as he had.

All her life she'd struggled. Hard work and grit were her keys to making things happen and getting ahead in life. She didn't regret that, either.

Still, she wondered how the other half lived.

"I can't believe you don't already have a date for the gala." An awful thought occurred to her. "You're not canceling on the blonde just to keep me out of the rodeo, are you?"

Although, remembering the way the woman had peeled out of the driveway with no regard to poor Carmen, Frankie found it hard to empathize with her.

"Blonde?" He sounded genuinely perplexed as he gestured toward his big black pickup.

"The one who startled my horse," she reminded him as he opened the passenger-side door for her. "Not that it's any of my business."

She waited to step inside the truck, more curious than she had a right to be about his answer. Surprised he didn't know who she meant.

"Her name is Kenzie, and no, she was never my date for the gala." He still held the door for her.

How very interesting. Did that mean he was currently unattached? Not that he ever seemed to date anyone for long. She'd seen a lot of women come and go in Xander's life in the months that she'd had a crush on him.

"Don't you think it will be awkward for you to take me? Since I'm—you know— a ranch hand?" A trace of misgiving crept through her.

"Not at all." He offered her his hand to help her up, clearly impatient to be under way. "There's enough drama brewing in the Texas Cattleman's Club without anyone worrying about who I bring to the party."

Ignoring his hand to pull herself up into the truck cab—mostly because she was extremely aware of the effect his touch had on her—Frankie mulled over his words. She hoped he was right. And yet another tiny piece of her wished that it wasn't easy for him to brush aside their evening together so casually.

What would it be like to attend the party with him? she wondered. Would it be like a real date? Or would she simply be circulating through the party on her own once he got her through the door?

It was one thing to be brave about riding a bucking bronc. At least then, you knew what you were getting. Facing Xander's peers at a fancy party had the potential to be more humiliating than landing on her butt in the dirt. What did she really know about him other than his reputation for never staying with any woman for long?

Stealing a sideways glance at him as he got behind the wheel of the truck, Frankie promised herself to keep a rein on her attraction to him tomorrow night. To simply enjoy the event she'd been wanting to attend so badly.

Because letting herself think for a moment that Xander Currin noticed her as anything more than a troublesome employee would only lead to heartache and disappointment. Now that she knew he was prone to chauvinism and arrogance, it ought to be easy to quit crushing on him.

Except the truck hadn't even pulled out onto the main road before she was already imagining what it might feel like to be in his arms for a dance.

Crisis averted.

Xander tried to tell himself he'd done the right thing as he steered his pickup onto the highway back to Currin Ranch. He'd ensured Frankie wasn't competing in a dangerous event, and now he was delivering her safely to her cabin on his family land.

But while the country love song crooning on the radio filled the truck cab, he couldn't deny that in dodging one disaster, he may have set himself up for another. Because no matter that he'd told her it wasn't a big deal to take her to the Texas Cattleman's Club Flood Relief Gala tomorrow night, he knew plenty of people would talk. Not that he gave a rat's ass about his own reputation, but he didn't like the idea of anyone giving Frankie a hard time. Rumors spread fast in the tight-knit ranching community.

He wasn't sure how to address that, so he tried to focus on the positive of what he'd accomplished. He kept his eyes on the road, knowing it was better to concentrate on that and the drive home than let himself think about the undeniably appealing cowgirl in the passenger seat.

"Do you mind if I change the station?" Her voice slid through his thoughts, her hand hovering over the radio dial.

His gaze flickered briefly from her fingers to her profile silhouetted by a streetlamp.

"Suit yourself." Damn, but she was pretty. Even after he'd returned his attention to the view in front of the headlights, he could still see her dark braid resting on her shoulder and tied with a blue ribbon.

She wore a bright blue Stetson he'd never seen before, and a brown suede vest over her turquoise-and-yellow-plaid Western shirt. The feminine touches didn't quite soften the proud tilt of her chin or the stubborn set to her jaw, but the contradictory side of her claimed his interest just the same. A ranch hand willing to risk her neck in the arena for the sake of a gala ticket.

"Thanks." Spinning the radio dial, she found a more fast-paced, rock-inspired country song and turned up the volume.

To avoid conversation? Fine by him. He didn't want to think too long about what he was getting into by accompanying her tomorrow night. And he sure as hell didn't want to contemplate the attraction he felt for her. She worked for him and that made her off-limits. End of story.

But she broke the silence between them just a moment later, turning down the volume again as he pulled off the interstate onto the dark county route that would lead back home.

"You mentioned there was a lot of drama in the Texas Cattleman's Club." She shifted in her seat to turn slightly toward him, her elbow resting on the console between them.

Close to his.

"Did I?" He'd never had any use for gossip, so he hadn't paid much attention to the rumors. But his father had been so involved with opening a branch of the TCC in Houston, it was impossible not to overhear things.

"You said no one would think twice about you bringing a ranch hand for a date tomorrow night because there was a lot of other drama brewing." Her voice had a soft huskiness that made him think of morning-after pillow talk and shared confidences. "What's that about? Anything I need to be aware of?"

He glanced her way again, her green eyes fixed on him with a warmth he couldn't ignore.

Better to talk about the TCC than dwell on the spark of awareness growing between them. Besides, he had to admire her quick mind and her willingness to prepare for the social outing.

"I'm sure you've read about the badly decomposed body found at the construction site where the Houston branch is being renovated." He straightened in his seat, putting some more distance between him and the intriguing woman beside him. "Having a murder victim linked to the TCC has everyone... anxious."

His father hadn't said much about it, but Xander guessed his dad must have some suspicions. Ryder Currin knew everyone involved in getting the Texas Cattleman's Club Houston branch off the ground.

"I read all the articles about that," Frankie mused, her finger tracing the leather stitching along the side of the console. "It seems like they're not speculating much while they try to identify the body."

"No one is speculating in an official capacity, but believe me, there's plenty of talk.

Some people think the victim could be Vincent Hamm, an assistant on the executive floor at Perry Holdings, who vanished into thin air right before the flood."

"Has anyone tried to locate him?" She went still, a note of alarm in her voice.

"Apparently his family told police he's always been a loner. He hated his job and often spoke of disappearing to a Caribbean island to be a surfer." He hadn't meant to worry her. "Maybe he finally did just that."

She fell quiet again, peering out her window as he passed a slow-moving farm vehicle.

"I did something like that once," she said after a long moment.

She surprised the hell out of him with the turn in conversation. He needed to stay on his toes around this woman.

"I can't picture you leaving it all behind to take up surfing." Although then again, she seemed to have a daring streak.

"Definitely not." She laughed, the sound

bringing a rush of pleasure that made him want to hear it again. "I meant that I took off from home a long time ago and never looked back."

A chill went through him and he glanced over at her again. "I hope no one hurt you back home."

"No. Nothing like that." She brushed aside the worry quickly, and she sounded sincere. "My parents treated me well enough, but they weren't my real parents, and I always felt like they'd hidden something from me about the day they found me."

She went on to explain how her parents had found her as a toddler, abandoned on a highway outside Laredo. They'd raised her as their own but had always been cagey about the circumstances of her arrival into their lives and what steps they'd taken—if any— to find her real parents.

"They were kind to me, but something always felt off about it." She lifted one shoulder in a shrug that looked more pained than casual. "Anyway, your mentioning Vincent

Hamm's possible decision to leave everything behind made me think of my hometown. I wonder what my friends and parents thought happened to me after I took off."

"I don't know, but I'm sorry you went through that." He wondered what had made this driven, fierce woman decide to turn her back on the people who raised her. There was probably more to that story, and he was curious, but he refused to pry when he was only just starting to know her. "I wish you could meet my sister, Maya. My father adopted her when she was a baby, and as far as I know, he's never told anyone how she came into his life."

"Seriously? How old is she?" Frankie steadied herself as the truck bounced over a pothole near the turnoff for the main house.

"She's eighteen and away at college. My dad was supposed to tell her the whole story once she reached adulthood, and Maya is more than a little upset he hasn't done that yet."

Xander clicked on his high beams as the

truck reached the wooden archway bearing the Currin Ranch sign.

"I hate secrets." The passion behind her words was obvious.

"That makes two of us." He'd had his own issues with secrets and surprises, and he sure as hell didn't plan to tread down that path again. He steered past the bunkhouse where a lot of the younger guys slept and headed toward the cabins. "But I'm guessing my dad has good reasons for keeping his. Maybe your parents are trying to protect you somehow."

"Maybe." She didn't sound convinced. "Anyway, thanks for the ride home."

She was tugging at her seat belt before he even had the truck parked. Because she wanted to escape his company? Or was she trying to ignore the same spark that kept drawing his gaze over her way?

"You don't have to thank me. I know this wasn't the ending you wanted for your evening." He switched off the truck to walk her to her door.

"It's fine," she rushed to say, already opening the truck door. "I can see myself inside."

He reached across the cab to put a hand on her forearm. "Frankie, wait."

Touching her had been a mistake—he knew it as soon as soon as his fingers landed on her sleeve. They wanted to linger there, to glide up her arm and around her shoulder to draw her closer. But he could hardly yank his hand back like he'd gotten scalded without revealing just how damned much she affected him.

So he let his fingers rest lightly where they were.

"I was hard on you tonight. Let me at least walk you to your door so I can tell myself I made an attempt to be a gentleman."

"You're my boss, not a gentleman," she argued, then frowned. "That came out wrong. What I mean is—"

"But as you pointed out earlier, we're not on the clock tonight." His fingers grazed her bare skin on the underside of her wrist, a surprisingly tender spot where he could feel her pulse thrum fast.

Her green eyes were wide in the glow of the dome light.

"Right." Her voice was all rasp and no substance. She cleared her throat. "Okay."

He slid his hand away and stepped out of the truck, walking around to her side.

He reached up to help her down, but she hopped out on her own. Wary of his touch? Or stubbornly proud?

Maybe a little of both. She was an intriguing woman.

"Thank you." She chewed her lower lip and peered up at him in the moonlight. "What time will I see you tomorrow?"

His gaze zeroed in on her mouth, his own suddenly dry as dust.

"I'll pick you up at seven." He was already questioning the wisdom of this bargain he'd made with her.

If she was affecting him this much now, what would it be like tomorrow night when they had a whole evening together? Already, the memory of the feel of her made his hands itch to touch her again. He hadn't thought this through well at all.

She nodded, her dark braid sliding down her shoulder. "And just so I'm clear, will we be off the clock tomorrow, too?"

Was she flirting with him? Or was he reading too much into it because he wanted her?

The tension of holding himself back was quickly knotting his shoulders, and they'd been together less than an hour.

"I'm going to let you make that call. You can tell me how much of the evening you want to be business and how much should be—" he couldn't think of any way to say it that didn't sound like a come-on "—pleasure."

She must have heard it, too, because her lips parted in soft surprise.

"Good night, Frankie." He was already imagining her in an evening gown and liking what he saw.

He played a dangerous game letting his

thoughts wander there, but he'd be damned if he could stop himself.

And with a silent nod, she pivoted on her boot heel and disappeared inside her cabin.

Three

Frankie finished her work as fast as possible on the afternoon of the gala, knowing she'd need extra time to get ready. She'd worked on the irrigation system most of the day, and had the dirty boots, jeans and face to prove it.

No doubt her hair was a hot mess under her hat, too.

Anticipation fired her movements as she returned one of the ranch's all-terrain vehicles to an overflow bay in the mansion's garage. She left the keys in the ignition, noticing that Xander's pickup was there, but his sports car wasn't. She hadn't seen him at all around the ranch during the day, but he'd told her he'd pick her up at the cabin at seven.

Which left her less than two hours to get ready.

At least she didn't have to spend any time choosing a dress, since she had only one possibility in her closet. Her lone black cocktail dress seemed like a boring option for an event like the gala, but it would have to suffice. Striding across the big horseshoe driveway toward her cabin, she noticed a sleek white Mercedes coupe parked in front of the main entrance of the Currin home.

As she neared the vehicle, the tall oak door of the house opened and Annabel Currin, Xander's half sister, stepped out onto the porch. She carried an armful of dresses— turquoise silk and emerald satin hems peeking from beneath the plastic bags with the name of a pricey local boutique.

"Those look like some gorgeous gowns," she called to her. She didn't know Xander's sister well, but Annabel had always been nice to her.

Tall and willowy, Annabel had been doubly blessed in the beauty department thanks to her Kenyan mother, Elinah, and movie-star handsome father, Ryder Currin. Frankie had seen photos of the couple before Elinah's passing, and Xander's stepmother had been stunning. Annabel favored her mom, with high cheekbones and dark brown eyes.

"Don't make me second-guess myself!" Annabel warned her with a laugh as she rushed down the steps toward her car. "I decided to keep the yellow one for the gala tonight, but it was a tough call because I love them all. I was just loading these up to donate tomorrow."

Frankie knew that Annabel was a local fashion and style blogger and often received samples from designers.

"Do you mean to tell me these are the rejects?" Frankie slowed her step as she neared Annabel's car. A fresh pang of worry about the dress code hit her. "Do you think a cocktail dress will be okay for tonight, or will I feel really underdressed if I don't have a gown?"

"You need a gown?" Annabel's eyes widened. "You're going to the gala?"

Frankie nodded, her anxiety doubling. "A cocktail dress is the wrong choice, isn't it?"

"You can wear one of these! No need to return it, even. I'll bet you are exactly my size." Annabel looked her over.

She felt self-conscious, knowing that she'd never worn an article of clothing as fine as the dresses in Annabel's arms.

"That's far too generous," she demurred. "I couldn't possibly—"

"Nonsense." Annabel clamped a hand on her wrist and tugged her toward the steps. "Cowgirl makeovers are my specialty."

Was she serious? Frankie had seen a few makeovers on the successful blog.

"Annabel, I'm a mess." Trepidation growing, she followed her onto the porch and through the front door, into the Currin family's home, which was more like a palatial Western retreat.

"That's why you'll make such a rewarding subject." Annabel headed straight for the grand staircase. "It will be fun."

"But you need to get ready, too." Frankie paused. "I don't want to be in your way."

"You won't be. I can get myself ready in ten minutes flat, if necessary." She shot her a level look. "Trust me, I timed myself and made a video for my beauty blog about paring down a routine when you're in a hurry."

Frankie laughed. "That's impressive. Okay, I'm game if you are. But I should take my boots off."

A few minutes later, they were in Annabel's huge suite. Frankie had stepped inside the Currin home before, but she'd never been past the foyer. Now she peered around Annabel's massive room in dove gray and off-white, the muted color scheme relaxing and peaceful. She listened to Annabel hum softly to herself while she hung the spare dresses on a narrow wall full of antique hooks near an old-fashioned changing screen. Then she reached into a shelf just inside the walk-in closet and emerged with a pink silk drawstring bag.

"Come with me." Annabel waved her toward an open door to the en suite bath. "There's an extra robe on the back of the bathroom door." She peeked behind the door to be certain. "And toiletries in here." She set down the pink silk bag on the marble vanity top. "While you shower, I'll think about what we can do with your hair. Sound good?"

Touched at the thought of Annabel opening her home to her, sharing an expensive gown with her and walking her through getting ready for such a special night, Frankie found herself at a loss for words. She feared if she tried saying thank you she would embarrass herself by bursting into grateful tears.

Nodding, she took refuge in the giant bathroom, surrounded by sleek white marble and pale gray tile accents. A bouquet of gardenias and white clematis spilled over a pewter vase, filling the air with fragrant notes. She washed up as fast as possible, making sure to remove all traces of Texas dust. When she was certain she was spotless, she toweled off with one of the fluffy bath sheets that Annabel had set out for her. Beside the towels, she saw the pink silk drawstring bag. Inside, she found pretty, barely-there underthings with tags still attached, along with a spare toothbrush and sample-sized toiletries. After brushing her teeth, she slid into the spare white robe.

When she opened the door to Annabel's suite, the space had been transformed. The recessed lights were on a dimmer, so that the bed and living area were now darkened. The brightest area of the room was now the corner that had been behind the changing screen. The painted screen had been folded aside to reveal an old-fashioned dressing table. The whitewashed French country piece had yellow and blue stenciled flowers on the drawers, and a round mirror was illuminated by wall sconces on either side. A small leather stool sat in front of the vanity.

"Are you ready for your makeover?" Annabel waved her deeper into the suite and Frankie noticed her hostess had applied her own makeup in the interim. "I've got your seat ready for you."

"I can't believe you're doing all this for me." As she dropped down onto the leather stool, she tried to articulate the gratitude that had seized her before the shower. "You're like a fairy godmother."

"This is fun for me," Annabel assured her. "I never really found my place on the ranch, but the style business suits me."

She talked a little more about her work in fashion and beauty blogging, then chatted about her fiancé, Mason Harrison, an executive at Currin Oil. Frankie found herself relaxing while she let Annabel dry her hair and set it in hot rollers, something Frankie had seen but never used.

"So who are you going to the gala with tonight?" Annabel asked once she'd moved on to makeup.

She tipped Frankie's face this way and that,

studying it in the light before reaching for a palette of colors in shades of cream to dark brown.

"Xander, actually." She explained about the rodeo and the deal they'd made. "So it's not like a date or anything. Just his way of making sure I didn't break my neck, I guess."

Annabel stiffened, dropping the compact she'd been holding.

"Annabel?" Frankie leaned forward to pick up the pretty red case with all the powders. "Are you okay?"

Had she said something wrong?

"I'm fine." The other woman seemed to force a smile. "Sorry about that, I just got distracted for a moment. You know, we should choose the gown before we do any more. So I can use the right colors for your face."

Was it Frankie's imagination, or had Annabel been in a hurry to change the subject? But since she didn't want to make her hostess uncomfortable, she hopped out of the chair to try on dresses. While she was in the huge closet—really like a room of its own, with a chandelier and padded window seat—trying on the first one, she could hear Annabel talking in the other room. When she emerged in the turquoise silk, however, Annabel was alone, texting on her phone.

She glanced up and gasped. "Oh, Frankie, that one is going to be the winner."

"Really?" She couldn't help a pleased smile. "I tried it on first because it was my favorite."

"It's a perfect color on you. I love the way it makes your eyes even greener." Annabel steered her in front of an antique cheval mirror. "What size are your feet?"

"Nine." She hadn't thought about shoes.

"That's Maya's size. She'll have something in her room to go with the dress, but I really think this one is the winner." She smoothed the hem and frowned down at Frankie's toes. "We'd better hustle if we want to get those toenails painted. Oh!" She gripped Frankie's forearm. "I almost forgot. Xander texted me about something else and when I mentioned you were here, he asked me to tell you that he's sending a car for you. His meeting ran late, but he'll have your ticket hand-delivered for you, and then Xander will meet you at the gala."

Frankie hadn't realized how much she was looking forward to seeing Xander tonight until that bit of news burst a hopeful bubble inside her. It was just as well that she keep in mind her Cinderella moment ended with her fairy godmother makeover. Xander wasn't really her date tonight, so she needed to focus on making contacts at the gala and enjoying just being there.

Romance wasn't on the agenda and the sooner she got it through her head, the better.

Xander waited for the meeting to end inside the specialty golf suite that his father had booked for the Texas Cattleman's Club VIPs to gather before the gala. He wanted to get out of here and find his date. He was looking forward to the night more than he ought to be, given that it was supposed to be an opportunity for Frankie to network. She had been in his thoughts far too often today.

For now, he was stuck in the golf suite. The Four Seasons in Houston had ballrooms to host the gala downstairs, but Ryder Currin had gathered his powerful friends ahead of time to discuss TCC business. The sports-themed suite upstairs contained a golf simulator like the pros used, and guests who weren't taking swings could relax on the leather couches or at a small bar. Normally, Xander didn't care much about golf, but he picked up a club now to try his luck at the simulator while his father continued to discuss last-minute details for the gala. He was restless and wanted to work out the edginess.

Lining up a shot on the green, Xander resented being here and dealing with local politics instead of escorting Frankie to what was most likely the first gala she'd ever attended.

Damn it, he hadn't wanted to meet her at the event, but he couldn't very well walk out of a meeting his father had asked him personally to attend. Ryder wanted Xander there in case his archrival, Sterling Perry, crashed the meeting.

The tension in his shoulders made him slice right, the ball bouncing into a water feature on the simulator's huge video screen. Continuing to play while the meeting got tense behind him, Xander heard his father arguing with someone about Sterling Perry. The two men had a history of enmity that started before Xander was born, so he didn't pretend to know all the nuances. There'd been rumors that Ryder had had an affair with Sterling's then-wife, Tamara. But Xander had never bought that. He figured Sterling just hated his dad because Ryder had once worked as a ranch hand for Tamara Perry's wealthy father, Harrington York, and inherited a small piece of property in that man's will. The property proved to be rich in oil and made Ryder a very wealthy man.

Sterling had resented the hell out of Xander's dad ever since, and the feud seemed to have taken on new life with the Texas Cattleman's Club opening a Houston branch. Both men wanted control, and Ryder's play to host the fund-raising gala tonight was probably a point in his favor.

Xander took a couple more swings, perfecting the shot he'd messed up the first time. But as he checked his watch and saw the time, he decided enough was enough for playing politics.

He was about to tell his father he was going downstairs to find his date when a woman entered the golf suite.

All of his father's cronies—eight men and a couple of women including his assistant, Liane Parker—stared as Angela Perry, Sterling's daughter, strode deeper into the room. Angela wore her long blond hair in a simple knot, her red dress simple and understated. Xander guessed she was under forty, though not by much, and she was already the executive vice president of Perry Holdings.

What the hell was she doing here?

He only had a moment to wonder about it when his father broke away from the rest of the group to stride toward her. He slid an arm around her waist and greeted her with a kiss on the cheek.

Well, holy hell.

"You look stunning," he overheard his father say.

Xander damn near swallowed his tongue, and he guessed the rest of the room did the same. Ryder Currin was dating Angela Perry, daughter of Sterling, the man he hated most in the world? Apparently his dad didn't practice what he preached about loyalty to blood and putting the family business first.

Returning his golf club to the rack near the simulator, Xander left the room to find his own date. Tonight was already getting off to a rocky start. But he still had something to look forward to this evening. Because he couldn't wait to see Frankie. He hadn't felt this pumped about a date since—

His heart hitched at the thought of Rena.

He pushed the thought aside. This didn't have to be complicated. He could just enjoy the moment. The date.

The woman.

Ten minutes later, entering the gala space glowing with candlelight from standing wrought iron fixtures, Xander searched the room for Frankie. He scanned past some of the Perry Holdings bigwigs, including Tatiana Havery and her brother laughing together, and a few ranchers he recognized at the bar.

Xander had almost given up finding her when... He did a double take.

Frankie?

Frankie.

She stood out in her turquoise gown all the more since she lingered with her back to a wall of bright fuchsia orchids. The Flood Relief Gala theme was "Blooming through Adversity," so flowers of all kinds filled the Four Seasons ballroom, but she outshone them all. Frankie's dark hair curled in soft waves around her face, so different from the functional ponytail she wore every day for work. Faceted crystals dangled from her ears, almost skimming her bare shoulders. Two delicate straps held up her close-fitting silk gown adorned with sequins, the shape fitted until it flared around her knees, mermaid style.

More beautiful than any woman in the room, she turned heads all around her as the orchestra launched into a slow song. The lights dimmed, and in his peripheral vision, he noticed couples take to the dance floor. But Xander couldn't take his eyes off Frankie as she clutched a tiny silver bag between both hands. She peered about the gala, as if looking for someone.

Him, no doubt.

He kicked himself for not getting down here sooner.

Pulled to her, he wished he'd brought her flowers. Done anything to make this evening more romantic and memorable for her. Because he couldn't deny it any longer. He wanted Frankie Walsh, and pretending otherwise wasn't going to make this keen need to have her disappear.

He snapped off an orchid bloom from a display spilling out of a silver urn near an ice sculpture of the new TCC building. He carried it over to her, his eyes holding hers every step of the way until he reached her.

"You look…incredible." He lifted her hand and brought it to his lips, lingering while her startled gaze collided with his.

Her eyes were deep green, like a lush field of spring grass. Her mouth was painted a bright shade of rosy pink, making him crave a taste of her. The scent of her skin—peaches and roses—stirred a deeper hunger.

"May I have this dance?" He tucked the bloom behind her ear, wondering how she'd managed the transformation from muddy cowgirl to exotic society beauty. He'd always found her attractive, but that attraction had been one-dimensional. Seeing this side of her, too, made her come to life in a multi-faceted way that rivaled the earrings grazing her shoulders.

No one would ever guess she'd spent half the day digging out a leaking irrigation system for repairs. Or that he'd had to stop her from entering a bronc riding event just the night before.

How many more hidden depths did this woman have?

"Yes, I'd love to dance." Her quick agreement, softly spoken, gave no hint of the strong, stubborn will that lurked beneath this delicate feminine guise.

Gratefully, he led her to the dance floor, wrapping her hand in his, stroking his thumb lightly over the center of her palm while they walked. He set her purse on their reserved table along the way.

When he reached an empty corner of the hardwood floor, he took his time skimming his hand down her back until it rested in the center. The back of her gown was low-cut enough that his palm grazed bare skin above the zipper, the tantalizing feel of her filling his senses.

Her fingers rested on his shoulder and she looked him in the eye as he swept them into the dance, moving with her easily. He wasn't letting her go tonight if he could help it. Frankie Walsh had become too much of a distraction for him to pretend otherwise.

But first, he couldn't resist teasing her while they swayed together.

"I've never seen you here before. May I ask your name?"

Four

Seriously?

Frankie's step faltered.

She knew that Annabel had transformed her. From the magic of makeup that gave her smoky cat's eyes complete with winged eyeliner, to the elegant dress and jewelry, the makeover was complete. But she wouldn't have guessed she'd be unrecognizable. She felt a flare of irritation that Xander would dance with another woman when—as far as he knew—he hadn't even taken the time to find his date yet.

"Francesca," she answered coolly, giving him her full name, a pretty, feminine moniker she'd never believed suited her.

But if there had ever been a time when she felt like a Francesca, it was right now, wrapped in a handsome man's strong arms as he whisked her around the dance floor in this fairy-tale setting full of flowers. She wouldn't have guessed a big, muscular cowboy like him would be so effortless on his feet, but he was such a sure, commanding partner, she didn't even have to think about following him. Her feet moved with his, her body in tantalizing proximity to him at all times, as she was swept away by the music, the moment…the man.

The custom-fitted tux couldn't hide the lean muscle of his shoulders, arms and chest. She felt his strength as they swayed together. Her body hummed with awareness.

"And what do you think of the gala so far, Francesca?" Her name was a seductive sound on his lips, his head inclined toward her ear so she could hear the softly spoken words over the orchestra's lilting strings.

"It's beautiful," she admitted, grateful to be here even if her date didn't recognize her. "I've never seen anything so lovely."

Bright fuchsia flowers spilled from center-pieces and twined around the tall columns framing the orchestra box. Tiny white lights threaded through greenery-laden tables. Added candlelight from tall sconces gave everything a warm, dreamy glow. The fragrance of roses, hyacinths and orchids was a heady aroma.

"I have." He slowed his steps as the music came to an end. The rest of the dancers applauded the musicians while Xander tipped her chin up to see her better. "You are the loveliest woman here, Frankie."

Her breath caught and she couldn't deny the delight. "You did recognize me."

"Of course." A smile pulled at the corner of his lips. "I asked your name as a way to start the night fresh. I thought if we were strangers meeting for the first time, we could enjoy our evening together without worrying about what it means for our working relationship."

She took his hand as he led her from the dance floor, a bolt of pleasure tickling its way up her arm. "It would definitely be easier for me if I wasn't your employee for a few hours."

"And yet I know you wanted to be here in order to network." He paused near the massive ice sculpture of the TCC Houston building, a historic former luxury boutique hotel that fell into disrepair and was now being renovated for the clubhouse.

Frankie had been following all the news about it, intrigued by the power struggle between Ryder Currin and Sterling Perry, two of the wealthiest men in town.

"It will be a while before I have my veterinary degree since I haven't even started a program yet," she said wryly, plucking a strawberry from a nearby table of desserts. "So I don't necessarily *need* to network. I just wanted to see the Houston branch of the

Texas Cattleman's Club come together since I hope to serve these people with my practice one day."

"Nevertheless, I will introduce you to some of the club's key members. Would you like to eat first?" Xander gestured to the buffet full of desserts. "Our table is over there, where I left your purse before the dance. If you want to have a seat, I can bring us both plates."

"I'd like that. Thank you."

Moments later, they were seated at their reserved table with Ryder Currin and—Frankie couldn't believe her eyes—Angela Perry. Together. They barely had time for introductions, however, when Ryder asked his date for a dance.

Excusing themselves, the surprise couple moved toward the dance floor. Heads turned as they went, which told Frankie she wasn't the only one shocked to see them together.

She turned back to ask Xander about it, but she caught him staring at her in a way that scrambled her thoughts. Self-consciously, she patted her hair.

"I'm not falling apart, am I?" She hated to reveal her nervousness, but she didn't want to mess up all Annabel's hard work. "I'm having visions of my makeup smearing or my hair rebelling and standing on end—"

"No. I'm sorry." Xander shook his head. "I didn't mean to stare." His hand came up to her hair, pushing a few waves behind her shoulder. "I thought for a moment it was a tattoo on your neck."

She felt her cheeks heat. "It's a birthmark."

She wasn't embarrassed about it or anything. It was visible all the time at work when she had her hair up. But Xander's close regard made her far too aware of herself. Of him.

Of the heat that simmered between them.

"It's such a perfect crescent moon." He skimmed a knuckle along the spot below her right ear, his fingers brushing her dangling earrings. "But I will confess, it wasn't just the birthmark. I was also trying to reconcile the elegant woman I'm seeing with the hard-nosed wrangler who was ready to bronc ride her way to a ticket last night."

"I thought I was going to be Francesca tonight and not Frankie?" she teased, stirring her spoon through a crème brûlée in a tiny ceramic dish.

"I'm intrigued by both of you." His blue eyes held hers, and she felt desire smoke through her.

Her mouth felt too dry to answer.

She'd had a crush on Xander Currin for as long as she'd worked at his ranch. So no matter how much she told herself that romance was dead and that he wasn't the kind of man who wanted romance anyhow, she still hungered for his touch. His attention.

And yes, his kiss.

Surely she wasn't alone in feeling that attraction now? His touches lingered, as did his stare. She might work for him, and she might be just a ranch hand in his big, wealthy world, but she could read the signs of male interest well enough.

"That's good," she told him, gathering up

her courage. Or her foolishness. She didn't know exactly which it was that made her say, "Because we're both fascinated by you, too, Xander."

Something stirred in his gaze. Interest. Arousal. Whatever it was made an answering flame leap inside her. He had a way of looking at her that made her feel like the only woman in the room. A unique experience for her. Was it only because of the magic that Annabel had wrought?

He leaned close to her as the number of partygoers grew. He slid his arm along the back of her chair at their private table, now empty except for them. His fingertips rested lightly along her shoulder, a touch that made a pleasurable shiver tremble along her nerve endings.

"I've avoided you around the ranch because of this." He pointed vaguely back and forth between them. "This awareness. I noticed you long ago and have tried to make sure that our paths didn't cross more than necessary."

"You noticed me?" She sounded too eager. Too breathless. But she was genuinely surprised. Her appetite for the rich desserts vanished as a new hunger took its place. "I had no idea."

"I try to put forward my professional best at work. So having my attention linger on a beautiful woman on my team would be a bad idea." His voice rumbled, low and gravelly, the admission sending a thrill through her. "But I don't think there's any sidestepping it tonight."

He looked into her eyes, a current of understanding passing between them. Her gaze dipped to his mouth and she found herself thinking about what it would be like to kiss him. A flush crept up her face, heat flaring over her skin.

Startled by the vividness of the things she imagined, she sucked in a breath while Xander traced one thin strap of her gown. The pads of his fingertips glided up the silk, leaving chill bumps in their wake.

"Definitely no sidestepping it tonight," he

mused, seeming to answer his own unspoken question. "Why don't I introduce you around the room so we can take care of business before we continue this far more interesting line of discussion?"

"Thank you." She nodded, pushing aside the china plate of decadent desserts he'd brought her. "I'd like that."

It would buy her time to think about what to do next. With her pulse racing and her thoughts full of Xander Currin, she needed a mental time-out to be sure of her next move.

As she took his hand and let him lead her toward an elegant-looking older couple taking a breather from the dance floor, Frankie went on social autopilot for the introductions. While she smiled and asked questions about their animals, Frankie was thinking about Xander all the while. Should she take the leap and give herself over to the attraction? Or keep fighting it for the sake of...what? Her job?

She wasn't worried about that. Xander was too honorable a man to make things awkward for her at work in the aftermath of whatever happened tonight. He'd avoided her before; he could avoid her again.

Her heart? She couldn't pretend she didn't have feelings for Xander. But she knew all too well from her close observation of him over the last year that he wasn't the kind to get attached. Surely she was smart enough to recognize that a love-'em-and-leave-'em guy wouldn't suddenly become a one-woman man after one night.

But as Xander slid an arm around her waist and introduced her to a rancher from the original TCC in Royal, Texas, who'd made the trip to Houston to support the new branch, Frankie knew she'd be hard-pressed to walk away from the temptation of even just one night with her sexy boss.

The attraction was so intense it was distracting when she needed to be focused on making enough money to afford veterinary school. On remembering the people here tonight so she could foster those connections down the road. She really did hope to have a mixed animal practice in the area. Or maybe a large-animal specialty. Yet she found it impossible to stay focused with Xander's touch making her so aware of him. Maybe indulging one fantasy evening in Xander's bed would finally excise him from her thoughts, freeing her to focus on her dreams?

Possibly she was simply rationalizing what she really wanted to do. But tonight, with the charismatic rancher beside her and the magic of her Cinderella transformation at work, Frankie couldn't deny herself the chance to follow the attraction wherever it might lead.

Xander knew he couldn't just tuck her under his arm and flee the gala with Frankie Walsh. But two hours after her revealing admission that she was "fascinated" by him, he still couldn't will away the desire for her that plagued his every move.

Now he pulled her onto the dance floor once more, wanting to be sure she enjoyed herself. She'd been willing to risk her beautiful neck for a ticket to this party, so he wasn't going to deprive her of the full gala experience just to indulge his personal desires. He'd introduced her to all the most prominent ranchers, giving her time to voice her goals of opening a veterinary practice in town once she completed her schooling. She'd received two offers to spend time in the barns if she needed more hours of animal time for her admission—something he hadn't known was required for her program.

He'd also learned that she volunteered most of her free time to shadow a local vet or to work at an animal shelter.

"Frankie, I hope you know you can ask for more hours in the barns at Currin Ranch." He hadn't meant to talk business with her when they were alone, but he didn't like the idea of other ranchers trying to lure her away with better positions. "I hate thinking you spent the day on that irrigation system when you need hours with animals in order to be admitted to veterinary school."

She was already shaking her head, a few

dark tendrils of hair twining around her dangling earrings as she moved.

"I'm not the kind of worker who requests special treatment," she insisted. "I have low seniority right now, so I'm willing to take the work that comes with that."

He wanted to know more about her. Where she got her work ethic, what inspired her to be a vet and why she would take foolish chances bronc riding when she had a bright future ahead of her. His gut knotted at the memory of how it had made him feel when he was trying to talk her out of it. His fiancée had been wearing a riding helmet when she fell during a jump, but that hadn't prevented her from hitting a fence post awkwardly.

"But you've been with us for nearly a year. It's not special treatment to share your work goals with your direct supervisor." He would make sure she was more involved in the barns. "We want you to remember us well when you've got your degree."

"I will." Her feet followed his, the hem of her gown sliding against his pant leg as he twirled her. A seductive whisper of touch. "I'll never forget what you did for me tonight, Xander. Meeting so many successful ranchers, getting to see the new Texas Cattleman's Club forming, I can't tell you how much that means to me."

One of her hands rested on his shoulder; the other was folded inside his. She wasn't nearly close enough to him. It was all he could do to keep his own palm steady on her back when what he really wanted was to skim a touch down the curve of her hips and pull her to him.

"Does that mean you've enjoyed your evening?" He liked seeing the way the candlelight brought a warm, burnished glow to her dark hair.

As for the pink in her cheeks, he'd like to think he put that there.

"It's even more beautiful than I imagined a fancy gala would be." She peered around the ballroom still packed with men in tuxes and women in gowns of every shade. "Seeing the world of the Texas Cattleman's Club is going to motivate me even more."

"What made you want to be a vet?"

"I think I first fell in love with animals when I saved a baby bird from a neighbor's cat." She smiled at the memory. "My parents homeschooled me and wouldn't allow me to join any local sports teams or—" she shook her head, the smile vanishing "—or any kind of club, really. I didn't have a lot of human companionship, but they were good about letting me keep strays. I survived some lonely years because of my animal friends."

"Like what?" he pressed, wanting to see her talk about happy memories. "I assume you kept the bird, for starters?"

"Not for long." Her smile returned. "I only kept the bird until he was strong enough to fly again."

"So what other strays did you take in?"

"Cats were a constant." Her voice was more enticing than the music, and he found himself wanting to listen to her talk at length about most anything. "I always fed at least ten cats every day, and considering the price of cat food, that necessitated a paper route."

"Industrious of you."

"Thank you. Over the years there were a handful of snakes and lizards, a very big iguana, assorted squirrels and chipmunks, two deer—"

"You had deer?" He'd underestimated her passion for the local wildlife.

"One was a doe that had a near miss with a hunter. The other was an abandoned fawn that I only kept until I was sure how to release her successfully back into a herd."

He was enjoying her story of rehabilitating a bat when the music came to an end, shifting to a more up-tempo song. Xander drew her to a quieter corner of the room.

Or it was until a woman's voice rose in volume at the table behind them. He turned in time to see Angela Perry glaring at her twin sister, Melinda. With blond hair and blue eyes like Angela, the two definitely resembled each other even though they weren't identical. Right now, however, they appeared unhappy with each other.

Angry, even.

"Seriously?" Angela clenched her fists, not even bothering to lower her voice. "How dare you question my romantic choices when you're dating a *mobster*!"

Melinda paled.

Xander searched the crowd for his father and didn't see him. He guessed Angela's first public appearance with Ryder Currin wasn't making her family happy.

"He's not a mobster!" Melinda shot back, her eyes blazing. "For your information, he just has mob *ties*." She snatched up her beaded handbag from the table and stormed off, leaving Angela alone.

Looking devastated.

Xander hated to pretend he hadn't overheard them, but wouldn't that be the most polite thing to do?

Frankie appeared ready to offer some words of comfort to Angela, taking a step in that direction. But at the same time, Ryder came striding through the crowd toward his date, two champagne glasses in hand and a concerned expression on his face.

No doubt his father would remedy the situation. Or try to.

"Let's go," Xander urged Frankie, wrapping his arm more securely around her waist. He noticed several people turning to stare at Angela as Melinda left the event in a huff.

Or were they turning to look at someone else? There was a lot of movement in the crowd suddenly.

"Out of my way," a man shouted right before Xander spotted Sterling Perry hurtling through the partygoers in the direction of Ryder and Angela.

"Damn," Xander muttered under his breath, regretting the turn of events on a night that he wanted to make special for Frankie. He'd been enjoying his time with her. "As much as I'd like to whisk you away from here right now, I need to make sure there's no bloodshed. Or arrests."

He didn't trust Sterling one bit, and the

man looked ready to spit nails despite his polished boots and the heavy silver bolo tie he wore with his flashy tux. He stopped a few feet from his daughter, where she stood beside Ryder.

For his part, Ryder looked unflustered, his expression patient. Xander guessed his father had faced down Sterling this way plenty of times over the years.

"I wouldn't believe it if I didn't see it with my own eyes," Sterling shouted at them while half of the party turned to see what was going on. "Bad enough this rat bastard undermines me by throwing a gala on behalf of a club he isn't even in charge of, but now my own daughter betrays me by—"

He halted midsentence, as if he was too angry to think of what he wanted to say. A hush fell over the gala guests nearby, everyone waiting to hear and making no secret of it.

"I've done nothing of the sort," Angela told her father in a more subdued voice. She sounded composed, but Xander noticed the white-knuckled hold she had on her champagne glass.

"If you don't stop seeing this upstart ingrate Currin, I'll cut you out of the company," Sterling threatened his daughter, leaning forward with his big shoulders. "Just see if I won't."

Xander was ready to jump in if needed, his muscles tense. This wasn't turning out to be the fun evening out he'd hoped to offer Frankie. The whole Perry family seemed to be angry with one another. And Sterling was angriest of all.

Ryder put a hand on Angela's back and spoke softly to her alone. Angela shook her head sadly. At least twenty people nearby strained harder to listen.

"I'm sorry, Ryder," she told him, setting down the crystal champagne flute right before she retrieved her small purse. "But I think it's best if I leave."

"Just like that?" Ryder's gravelly voice was pitched low, but Xander still heard him. "You're going to let him dictate what you do?"

His father was angry. Xander could see it in the way he held himself, even though to the rest of the world he might appear composed. No doubt, he'd put himself on the line to bring Angela with him here tonight. To have her walk away so publicly had to upset him.

But that's just what Angela did, taking Sterling's arm as the two of them left the gala together.

Xander could have sworn the musicians played louder, as if the whole place conspired to be more festive so the party could continue. He empathized with his father, knowing the pain of having a woman surprise him that way. Rena's shocking news before her riding accident had haunted him long afterward.

Old regrets of his own churned.

"Should you talk to your father?" Frankie asked, laying a gentle hand on Xander's tux sleeve while they watched Ryder disappear into a private room in the back. "He looks upset."

Xander forced himself to let go of his own demons, knowing this wasn't the time for bad memories.

"I think he'd prefer to be by himself." Xander recognized that set to his dad's shoulders, the stress of the night weighing on him. "I'll check in with him tomorrow. Right now, I'm more concerned about you. This isn't how I wanted to end the evening. It's your call if we stay longer or call it a night."

For his part, he knew what he preferred.

He'd wanted Frankie alone ever since he'd first spotted her in front of that wall of flowers.

"As much as I hate for the night to end, I guess I'm ready to leave." She took a party favor—a silver horseshoe charm—from one of the tables near the door. "I'm going to take this as a memento, though. It's so pretty."

Her quick smile at the gift charmed him.

For that matter, her simple appreciation of the token made him feel jaded to think how many functions like this he'd attended over the years, how many party favors he'd walked right past without even noticing them. Frankie looked at the evening in a much different way. Was it selfish of him to want to keep her with him longer, to see the world through her eyes for a little while?

And yes, he wanted her close in every other way, too.

So he wrapped his arms around her, drew her near to tell her what he'd been wanting to say all evening long.

"Keep in mind, just because we leave the party doesn't mean the night has to end."

I sip my whiskey slowly, savoring the taste. The hundred-year-old brew is smooth, mellow and delicious, but it can't compare to the thrill of another satisfying night's work. Standing at the back of the Flood Relief Gala, I can't help but savor how well things went tonight in my plan for revenge. I hate Sterling Perry and Ryder Currin for what they've done to me. For everything they've stolen and ruined in my life. But things are starting to turn in my favor. Every day, I get closer to bringing them down and making them feel my pain. Tonight, Sterling Perry was so angry he was breathing fire when he saw his daughter with Ryder Currin. I thought he might keel over from the fury!

And Ryder didn't fare much better in all the drama. His date walked out on him in front of the whole Texas Cattleman's Club. The man hides his emotions a whole lot better than his rival, but of course he felt humiliated. Who wouldn't have been?

So much success to savor, and I hardly had to lift a finger.

Now, I just have to keep my eye on the prize. Once Angela Perry discovers the information I planted about Ryder, she's sure to cut him out of her life forever.

As for Sterling? His good reputation is about to crash and burn.

Five

Frankie had driven through the front gate to Currin Ranch many times. But when Xander slowed his luxury coupe in front of the six-foot stone pedestals that held the wooden arches for the ranch's welcome sign, the electronic sensor swinging the gates open, she acknowledged that her arrival felt very different this time as a guest.

Xander's guest.

Back at the gala, he'd made it clear the night didn't have to end when they left the party. She'd understood that the invitation meant they might well end the night in bed. Now, as he steered the vehicle through the gate and down the main drive toward the mansion, she knew it was up to her to make it clear what she would like to happen next.

She knew what she *wanted*. She just didn't know if indulging her desires was wise. It had been fun learning a little more about her sexy boss and his world, even though he'd been very skilled at getting her to talk about herself more than the other way around. She didn't usually share details about her past like that—the way she'd grown to love the company of animals, or how she'd felt lonely as a kid because of her parents' isolating life-style.

But somehow, she'd shared all those things with him.

"Do you want me to take you to your cabin?" He glanced over at her, his face illuminated by the amber glow of dashboard lights. "Or stop at the ranch house for a drink?"

What she preferred was a kiss. And everything that went with it. But did she dare act on that inclination?

She hadn't come this far in life by backing down from what she wanted.

"My place is a bit of a disaster," she admitted. It was also very small and humbly furnished. "So if yours is an option, that might be better."

This was happening.

"Definitely." He pulled into the driveway and hit the button for one of the garage bays, the door yawning open at his approach. "The pool house is all lit up," he observed before driving inside the mammoth structure. "It's not too hot out tonight, if you want to sit outside for a little while."

"That sounds nice." And romantic. Tempting. She waited in the passenger seat after they parked, and he came around to help her out of the vehicle. "I wouldn't mind some fresh air."

She took his hand, unaccustomed to managing a gown and heels in a ballroom, let alone getting in and out of a low-slung sports car. Straightening, she followed him through a side door out onto the stone deck and around to the back of the pool house. The building had the same Western log style as the main house, one side full of floor-to-ceiling windows and a pair of French doors. Outside them, a patio table and cushioned loungers were half hidden by bright bougainvillea draped down from the red cedar pergola. Landscaping lights hidden in the surrounding trees and bushes made the pool area look like a nighttime oasis.

"I'll get us some drinks," he offered, releasing her hand to open the door.

"I'll help." She darted through ahead of him as he held the door for her. "Plus, I'm curious to see what a pool house looks like inside."

The Currin family's lifestyle intrigued her. She was happy with the cabin she lived in that was part of her compensation as a ranch hand, but walking into the Currin world was like opening a glossy magazine about the rich and famous. She didn't need that life, but it was beautiful to see.

Her childhood home had been tiny, an out-of-way converted barn with no neighbors for miles.

"My father isn't much for decor," Xander explained, gesturing to the huge open living space flanked by a bar on one side and a small kitchen on the other. "He's definitely from the 'less is more' school of thought."

"Annabel's suite wasn't like that. But I'm guessing she decorated that herself." She spun around in a circle as she strode deeper into the room. The natural stone floor was a nod to wet bathers, but other than that, it was graciously appointed. A leather sectional couch sat in front of a fireplace on the opposite wall.

While the space was furnished simply, everything was high-end and luxurious, from the silent spinning ceiling fans overhead to the heavy bronze accents around the fireplace and pendant lights over the gray quartz bar. The pendants were dimmed to a low setting, casting a muted golden glow in the room. It was brighter outside by the pool, but the tall windows let in some of that light, too.

"Annabel definitely put her personal stamp on her rooms. But the rest of the house is more stripped down. Have you ever seen the Perry place?" Xander asked as he poured two glasses of sparkling water. He returned the bottle to the refrigerator in the kitchen and then brought her a glass. "His ranch house looks more like a castle, so I guess I think of Dad's taste as fairly subdued."

"I've seen photos of Perry Ranch in the news, so I know what you mean. But this is beautiful in a different way. Understated can be lovely, too."

Standing near a sofa table, she peered around the room, admiring it a little longer, until her gaze collided with Xander's. Her skin heated.

He raised his glass, his eyes still locked on her. "Cheers to making it through your first gala."

Her heartbeat sped faster as she lifted her

glass. "Cheers to seeing the world I've been dreaming about with my own eyes. Thank you taking me tonight."

She took a slow sip, letting the cool water quench some of the fire rolling through her at the realization they were more alone than they'd ever been. The only sound was her breathing and the clink of ice cubes in their glasses.

"The pleasure was all mine." He set his drink aside on the sofa table. Then he took hers from her as she lowered it, and set that one down, too, balancing each one on a marble coaster. "I don't usually care about glitzy events like that, but I enjoyed being with you tonight."

Her throat felt dry already, even though she'd just had a drink. She stared up at him, mesmerized, aching for his touch.

"I've wanted to kiss you from the first moment I saw you tonight," he confided. Reaching toward her hair, he plucked the orchid bloom from behind her ear. She'd forgotten that he'd placed it there when he first walked up to her at the gala. Now he laid the delicate petals on the table, too, while her heart kicked harder against the inside of her chest.

She'd dreamed of him too many times in the months that she'd crushed on him. It hardly seemed possible she'd fantasized this moment into reality.

"You have?" Her voice was a breathless squeak of sound, but she was determined to claim this one night with him. Or however many nights he was prepared to give her. So she forced herself to make her feelings more plain. "Then what are you waiting for?"

He stared down at her for an interminable moment before one knuckle brushed the underside of her chin, tipping her face toward his. Anticipation tingled over her skin. He angled closer and she breathed him in for an instant before his lips met hers. A tender brush of his mouth.

Sweet. Sensual. Tempting.

She went still under the onslaught of sensations. The scents of cedar and musk. The warmth of his hand sliding around her waist.

She all but melted against him, craving the feel of all that delicious male muscle. The silk of her dress slid between them in a teasing glide of fabric.

The kiss tantalized her, reminding her of all the times she'd imagined this moment, and all the ways her imagination hadn't done it justice. The reality of Xander was hotter. Harder. Hungrier.

Or maybe that last part was her.

Because when he deepened the kiss, she thought she might spontaneously combust. The press of his lips sent ribbons of pleasure through her. Her fingers were raking off his tuxedo jacket and wrestling with the buttons on his shirt, a feverish desire for more of him making her ache.

He broke away suddenly, his breath ragged as if he'd been running. "Hold that thought."

Pulling his hands from her waist, he moved toward the door and locked it. The bolt slid home in a welcome, satisfying sound. When he turned toward her again, she took in his shadowed jaw and newly rumpled silk bow tie thanks to her questing hands. Two buttons on his pleated tuxedo shirt were unfastened, giving her a tantalizing glimpse of his chest.

Her heartbeat echoed his footsteps, getting faster as he neared.

"Come with me." He took her hand and led her deeper into the pool house.

She hadn't noticed the archway off the kitchen earlier, but he led her through a nook where a coffee bar lined one wall and a wine cabinet the other. Then he opened a door to a guest bedroom. The white walls were offset by the gray stone fireplace at the foot of the bed and a gray planked ceiling that sloped under an exterior gambrel. A bed was tucked into the corner, the white comforter and gray leather headboard as understated as the rest of the room.

Behind her, Xander closed the door. Blinds covered the windows, and it was dark for a moment before he hit a switch to light a wrought iron lamp on the mantel. She slid out of her shoes while he disappeared into the bathroom, emerging a moment later with a foil packet that he placed on the cedar chest beside the bed.

He met her gaze. Waiting.

She recognized the moment for what it was—a chance for her to be certain this was what she wanted. The condom was a clear indication of his desires. Now it was her turn. And she didn't think twice.

With a roll of her shoulder, she shrugged off one strap of her gown. Then she slid a finger under the other strap and skimmed it down. Turning her back on him, she put the zipper in easy reach before she swiveled a look over one shoulder.

"A little help, please?" she asked, although she was so ready to be naked with him, she would have wriggled her way out of the dress if necessary.

He shifted closer behind her, his knee grazing her. He pushed aside the luxurious waves Annabel had created with her hair, baring her spine before he placed a kiss there. The shiver that tripped through her was pure pleasure.

Then he inched the zipper down. Silk fell in a sensual flow down her skin, the tissue-thin gown pooling at her hips. From behind her, Xander snaked one arm around her waist, nudging the fabric the rest of the way off.

"Wow." The soft word, reverently spoken, made her suddenly self-conscious.

She'd never been a woman who inspired that kind of reaction in men. Spinning in his arms, she faced him.

"Now I get to see you." She unfastened the next button on his shirt, pressing a kiss to his heated skin as she worked one after the other. Losing herself in the feel of him, the rapid tattoo of his heartbeat under her lips, the taut muscle of his abs as she neared his waist.

When she flicked open the hook on his trousers, he returned the favor by undoing her bra clasp. And while she still didn't trust her wow-factor, she enjoyed the gleam of appreciation in his eyes before he cupped a breast in his hand, thoroughly distracting her from undressing him.

She swayed on her feet, bracing herself by gripping his shoulders. Naked, hot, strong shoulders. Her knees wobbled even more until he walked her backward toward the bed, lowered her onto the downy comforter, then joined her there. The press of his hips against hers reminded her that the night was going to get so much better.

Desire fluttered along her feminine muscles, like a butterfly kiss, and they hadn't even gotten all their clothes off yet. Arching harder against him, she wanted more.

Now.

He obliged with a kiss to her breast, drawing on the nipple until the peak pebbled impossibly tighter. She tunneled her hands through his dark hair while he kissed and laved the other breast, and tension coiled tighter inside her.

"I'm so close. Please." She stroked her palm down his back, fingers combing aside the waistband of the tuxedo pants.

"You are?" He reared back to look down at her, his blue eyes a shade darker, the black centers wide. "You don't need to wait for me."

He reached between her thighs, cupping her through the tiny scrap of silk she still wore.

All that delicious tension stirred. She gasped from the pleasure of it.

"I can wait. I just—" She reached for the condom, but the nightstand was too far. "It just feels—"

He slid aside the silk and stroked circles right *there*, where she needed him most.

"I can't wait to make you feel good," he whispered in her ear, his lips brushing her cheek while he spoke, one of his legs pinning hers in the most pleasant way imaginable.

More than pleasant. It was sexy as hell.

And whatever he was doing with his hand felt so—

The building tension burst, her release hitting her hard and fast, the waves of oh-so-amazing fulfillment racking her body. Again.

And again. He seemed to know exactly how to make it last, touching her in ways that elicited every ounce of bliss from an orgasm unlike anything she'd ever achieved on her own or with help.

None of which she could articulate, since sparks still shimmered behind her eyes. Vaguely, she knew he'd stood up long enough to undress and retrieve the condom. By the time he dragged her panties off and stretched out over her, she was recovered enough to kiss him. To wrap her arms around his neck and stroke a caress up the hard, hot length of him.

To look in his eyes as he eased his way inside her, inch by delectable inch, filling her.

She wrapped her legs around him, holding him there while her body adjusted to him, and she tried to catch a breath. But looking up into the blue eyes she'd dreamed about too many times, she knew that probably wasn't going to happen. She was in bed with someone she'd fantasized about. Someone she'd never hold on to.

It was okay if she just sank into the moment. Closing her eyes, she gave herself over to the feelings and met his hips thrust for thrust, finding her own rhythm.

When he rolled her on top of him, she moved with abandon, letting her body take the lead, feeling the delicious heat build again. She staved it off by focusing on him. On kissing his neck. Nipping his jaw. Tipping her head to one side to drape her hair along his chest and drag it upward like a silken touch.

She knew he was close when he gripped her hips. Holding her where he wanted her. Guiding her. Only then did she give herself over to everything she was feeling. For the second time. When his muscles tensed everywhere, hers did, too. She flew apart a moment before him, his shout drowning out her soft cries as pleasure tumbled through her until she was wrung out from it.

She slumped to his side, holding him tight. Wanting to curl up against him and stay there forever.

Dangerous thoughts.

But she was too damned fulfilled to push the notion away. The aftershocks still trembled through her as their heartbeats slowed, their breathing synched.

While the spinning ceiling fan cooled her skin, she did exactly as she pleased and laid her head on his chest. If she only had one night with Xander Currin, she was going to make the most of every moment.

Xander knew he'd stepped over a line by sleeping with someone he employed. It had been unethical. Selfish. Shortsighted.

And he still couldn't scavenge up even the slightest regret about it.

Frankie had brought him something more valuable than physical pleasure tonight, although the sex alone had floored him. She'd also somehow given him a night of peace from his personal demons, and that was a surprise he wasn't ready to analyze. He combed his fingers through her hair in the quiet aftermath of lovemaking, savoring the stillness in his brain. The lack of guilt and grief that had dogged him after nights with other women.

How had she done that?

Or was it simply time for him to turn the page on his past for good? He tamped down those questions to focus on the woman beside him.

"Can I get you anything?" He twined a lock of dark hair around his finger, wanting to be thoughtful. Considerate.

Wanting her to stay longer.

"Clean skin." Glancing up at him, she grinned. "I've never worn makeup like this before and I'm scared I'll leave half my face on the pillow."

Gently, he traced one of the wings on her eyeliner where it slanted toward her temple.

"It still looks perfect." Her skin was so soft. "But if you come in the shower with me, I can promise you'll end up with a clean face. Eventually."

He could read the desire in her eyes as

she followed his thinking. Her fingers flexed against his chest.

"That sounds…ambitious of you." She walked her fingers down his abs. Lingered there.

Hunger for her stirred. Already.

"I aim to please." He slid off the bed and tugged her to her feet. "Besides, I already know what it's like to be with your exotic alter ego, Francesca. But I've got a serious thing for Frankie."

He pushed open the door to the guest bedroom's en suite bath and reached into the shower stall to flick on the water. Eight jets turned on at once, but he dialed off four of them to give them more options.

"I might need a putty knife," Frankie observed as she rubbed at a streak of gold-flecked shadow on her brow bone. "Your sister used something called makeup setting spray on my face. I didn't even know there was such a thing."

"Annabel is a beauty artist." He grabbed two washcloths, a condom and a bar of scented soap from the cabinet and set them on the teak shelf in the shower. "But in my opinion, you're even prettier without the wizardry."

Frankie turned away from the mirror, her eyebrows raised in surprise for a moment, before she shook her head. "Thank you. But Annabel made me feel worthy of the dress and the event, you know? Like my face was dressed up, too."

"Well, we're undressing you now. And I have to say, I've thoroughly enjoyed unveiling you tonight." He pulled her into the shower with him and she tipped her head back into the spray.

He took his time washing her—massaging shampoo into her scalp until her head tipped back against his shoulder. After rinsing out all the lather, he went to work with the washcloth, lingering in some areas. Behind her neck where she was exquisitely sensitive, and at the small of her back where touches made her shiver with pleasure.

Xander would have gladly denied himself

longer, enjoying the discovery of what she liked best. But when he teased the cloth just inside her hip bone one time too many, she reached for the other cloth and began her own sensual journey around his body. She used her lips, too, arousing him with hot, wet kisses while she massaged his skin with her fingers. Driving him to the brink with no more than that.

When he didn't want to deny either of them another minute, he tugged the terry cloth from her hands and tossed it on the tile floor along with his. Sheathing himself with the condom, he shielded them from the spray with his back. Her breath came in fast pants, her green eyes unfocused and desire-dazed. He parted her thighs and entered her in one stroke.

He lifted her higher until she wrapped her legs around his waist. Water sluiced over her while she arched into him, her hands splayed on his shoulders to steady herself, her head tipped back in abandon. There was something so uninhibited about her. So damned sexy.

He wanted to delay his release, but seeing her like this was more than his senses could take. He reached between them, trying to throttle back his needs for the sake of hers, stroking the sweetest center of her that elicited soft cries from her throat. Tiny moans. He felt the tension in her, too. Her back bowed harder, her ankles locking him in place.

The rapid pulse of her feminine muscles against him was the last straw, drawing him deeper. Finishing him. He gripped the partial wall of the shower to steady himself while pleasure pummeled him.

He didn't move for long moments afterward, not trusting his legs if he shifted his feet. Finally, she unwound herself from him with his help, until she stood on her own feet again. He'd never felt so damned good.

And with that thought, the guilt came crashing back over knowing he had nothing left inside him to offer a woman after losing Rena.

Fighting through it, he turned off the water and passed Frankie a towel, then grabbed one for himself. As they dried off together, he acknowledged that the bout of grief felt further away than normal. He might not have even experienced it this time if he hadn't thought about how damned amazing it felt to be with Frankie.

The best, a contrary part of his brain insisted.

All the while, he somehow carried on a conversation. He helped Frankie find a comb so she could untangle her hair. He urged her to lie down with him afterward, assured her that she didn't need to leave yet.

But he knew he'd checked out on her. The same way he had with other women ever since his fiancée died. What disturbed him was that this time, he hadn't simply enjoyed the sex for a temporary escape.

Tonight was different because he didn't want their time together to end. And considering that he had no plans to enter a real relationship again, Xander could tell things were about to get complicated.

Six

Back in bed an hour later, Frankie wouldn't let herself fall asleep.

Lying beside Xander under the covers, she listened to the sound of his breathing slow as she tried to figure out what had happened tonight. Something had shifted between them after the shower. Or rather, something had shifted for Xander afterward. She could practically feel him pull away from her in the moments after the incredible release. A tension had crept into his whole body. Whereas after the first time, he'd been just as relaxed as she in the aftermath.

Had she reached the time limit Xander seemed to put on all his relationships? It was like a stopwatch had gone off in his head telling him that he'd spent long enough with her. And that stung—hard—even though she'd known going into this that it would happen.

He'd continued to be kind to her, saying the right things, massaging her shoulders and finding a clean T-shirt and shorts for her to wear. But she could tell he'd checked out on her. Emotionally. Mentally.

So when his breathing grew deep and even, she slid from the bed and retrieved the beautiful gown and shoes Annabel had let her borrow. Her cabin was close, but the barn with the vehicles was even closer, so she borrowed a ranch pickup truck to drive herself home. She'd return it early in the morning anyway, because she didn't expect to sleep much after everything that had happened.

Her brain would be busy churning through all the details and trying to figure out what would happen next. She wasn't worried about her job, per se, because Xander was too honorable to make her work difficult for her. But she did worry how the rest of the ranch workers would treat her once word got around that she'd dated the boss. It would be awkward.

But somehow, she had to move forward now that she'd slept with a man she'd crushed on for the better part of a year. He shouldn't have the power to distract her from her future anymore.

Except she had the sinking feeling she was fooling herself about that. Because even now that the mansion lights were well behind her, she still caught herself looking back in the rearview mirror, thinking about what might have been if she could have spent the night.

The morning after the disastrous Texas Cattleman's Club Flood Relief Gala, Angela Perry woke to the sound of text messages on her phone. One chime after the other—all notifications from Ryder Currin.

Closing her eyes against the cheerful sound that she'd assigned to his messages, Angela burrowed deeper in the pillow of the guest suite at Perry Ranch—formerly her childhood bedroom. She'd ridden home with her father after the gala in an attempt to calm him down. He was so upset with her for daring to date Ryder that smoothing things over had taken the better part of the night. Instead of calling for a car to drive her back to her condo, she'd retreated to one of many vacant bedrooms at the ranch, gravitating toward the one that used to belong to her back when she, Melinda, Esme and Roarke had been raised here.

The house echoed now, with everyone gone but her father. Roarke had moved all the way to Dallas to escape the family. Esme and Melinda both lived downtown, like she did. Their mother had been gone for ten years now, and Angela missed her every day.

Being here wasn't the same anymore, but Angela had been too tired to argue with her dad last night. Besides, she had an ulterior motive by staying here.

Levering up on one elbow, she checked her phone and saw three texts from Ryder.

Does Sterling dictate who you date?

Last night didn't end the way I had hoped.

I'd like to speak to you in person.

Tension balled in her gut. She felt guilty about leaving the party without him last night, but she wasn't ready to face Ryder yet.

Not until she spoke to a neutral third party to learn whatever she could about Ryder's past with her mother. She'd heard the gossip that he'd had an affair with her mom, Tamara, back when Ryder had worked at Tamara's father's Ranch. There were rumors that Ryder had blackmailed her mother into convincing her own father to will Ryder the land that had made the Currin family wealthy.

Angela didn't buy it—not any of it. But her closest friend and a fellow Perry Holdings vice president, Tatiana Havery, had convinced her to ask around the ranch and speak with employees who'd lived here back when Ryder worked for Angela's maternal grandfather—Harrington York. To find out if any of them remembered seeing her mother and Ryder together in a way that seemed suspicious. In those days, the place hadn't been called Perry Ranch. Angela's father had changed the name from York Ranch after Harrington died.

Tatiana's advice had seemed wise, but then, it was no surprise Tatiana would look out for her since they'd been friends as far back as boarding school days. When they'd first met, the Havery family had been even more influential than the Perrys, and Angela had always appreciated Tatiana's blunt honesty. Now, taking her friend's advice, Angela would simply learn whatever she could for herself about Ryder's old friendship with her mother, and then she could move on.

Once she'd done that, then she'd answer Ryder's texts. Because if it was true that he'd had a secret affair with her mother long ago… Angela couldn't even contemplate that. Especially not now that she'd kissed him and the chemistry between them had been amazing.

Clutching her phone tighter, she forced herself out of bed because she knew whom she needed to seek out. One of the older ranch hands who'd been on staff forever and Carla, the maid who'd worked in the house the longest. Angela just needed to be discreet about questioning them because she couldn't afford to give her father any more reason to get riled about her relationship with Ryder.

There was no question Sterling Perry hated Ryder. But was it simple resentment that Ryder had made a fortune from land that Sterling had coveted for himself? Or did her father know firsthand that Ryder had had an affair with Angela's mother?

The sickening feeling in her belly grew worse. She couldn't imagine her mother having an affair, no matter how much Sterling ignored her. Tamara hadn't been that kind of woman, had she?

Angela believed her mother would have gotten out of her marriage before she did something like that. But then again, those rumors persisted.

One thing was certain, however.

She wasn't leaving Perry Ranch until she got some answers.

By noontime, Frankie hadn't seen any sign of Xander, but she told herself that was only because she'd been in the far west pasture all morning, checking and mending fence before they moved half the herd there next week.

As sundown approached and she still hadn't seen him around the barns, however, she guessed he was avoiding her.

Because he was angry with her for leaving while he slept?

Or would he simply behave as though last night had never happened—and go back to his old pattern of avoiding her?

She was repairing a gate to prevent one of the escape artist goats from opening the latch when Xander entered the paddock area. He'd always snagged her eye in the past with his lean, muscular build, his long-legged stride and those blue eyes clear as a Texas summer sky. But now that they'd been together and she knew what it felt like to be at the center of that azure gaze, the draw of his presence was almost impossible to resist. Could it have been any more obvious to her that spending one night with Xander hadn't cured her crush on him? It took a supreme act of will to straighten up from her work with a casual air.

"The gate is fixed." She demonstrated the new double-latching mechanism because she was nervous and didn't know what else to say to the man who was her boss but also her temporary lover. "No more late-night roaming for the goats."

"Thistle is getting ready to have her foal," Xander told her as he stalked past her, heading into the barn without slowing his step or giving more than a passing glance to the gate latch. "I told Len to schedule you in the barn tonight, and let him know you need more hours with the animals."

She tucked her screwdriver into a side pocket on her work cargoes and hurried after him. She didn't know what she was more excited about—being with the mare who was going through her first delivery, or having Xander's approval to log more time with the ranch's livestock.

Did that mean he wasn't upset with her? Or had he simply given her this boon because he was going to drop her like a hot potato after last night? She tried to steel herself for either scenario.

"Really?" She sidestepped a couple of barn cats asleep on the walkway. Apparently they were taking the afternoon off from hunting mice. "Thank you so much."

Once they neared the birthing stall, Xander toed the barn door shut behind them. No doubt to help keep Thistle isolated and calm for her first birth. Frankie had been around the barn for births of calves and kids, but never for one of the foals. And never for the whole delivery.

She'd assisted in plenty of other births while shadowing a local vet, but this was different. Special, somehow, because she knew these animals. She might just work here, but that connection sort of made them "hers," too. In her mind, anyway.

"You left last night." He faced her head-on, a stubborn set to his jaw as he stood in the shadows cast by the huge post beams holding up the roof. "Care to explain that?"

His eyes found hers even as she tried to adjust to the dimness. She could see the disappointment in his face. Hear it in his voice. Confusion knotted inside her. Had she misinterpreted his signals? She was so sure he'd pulled away from her.

"I didn't want to overstay my welcome," she told him carefully, surprised he was willing to bring up the private subject while they were working.

She wandered closer to Thistle, a pretty

buckskin quarter horse with sooty shading on her back.

The mare didn't seem agitated yet, nickering softly as Frankie rubbed her muzzle. The scent of fresh hay drifted up from the horse's hooves as the mare shifted her weight.

"Did I make you feel unwelcome?" Xander asked, keeping his voice low, probably out of deference to the soon-to-be mother.

Even so, the deep rumble sent an answering shiver through her as he ran a hand along Thistle's flank, most likely assessing the position of the foal.

"No." She'd felt very welcome. Also, she'd felt more sensually fulfilled than she'd known a woman could be. But she wasn't sharing that. "Maybe I just didn't want to face morning-after awkwardness."

How could she tell him she was scared he'd ditch her the way he did every other woman?

If he knew how closely she'd watched ladies come and go over the last eleven months, he'd realize that she'd been having feelings for him for a long time. Too long.

It was embarrassing and sort of cliché to have a crush on the boss, wasn't it?

"Right. Because this isn't awkward at all." Sarcasm laid heavy on the words, even though his gentle tone never changed as he straightened up.

"Do you honestly think me staying longer would have made today any different? It was going to be tense no matter what."

For her, anyway.

Maybe for him, working with someone he slept with wouldn't have been a big deal. But how long could she pretend to be the kind of woman he preferred—someone who was okay with a casual hookup? Then again, maybe she should try to become that woman. She needed her mind focused on getting into school, not mooning over a man.

When he didn't reply right away, she glanced over at him across Thistle's muzzle and realized he was studying her a bit too thoughtfully.

"I don't want to make things difficult for you here," he said finally. "Did anyone say anything to you to make today uncomfortable?" He took her hand to draw her out of the birthing area.

Her boots crunched over clean straw until they were back on the concrete floor outside the foaling stall. Xander pulled the door shut to help Thistle relax.

"No. I don't think word has gotten around that we attended the gala together." The whole night seemed like something she'd dreamed.

Except that she was standing in the barn with Xander today, and he'd given her new responsibilities that would help her on her path to vet school. She appreciated that he took her dreams seriously. That he would try to help her achieve her goals.

"Even if gossip does spread, why should it matter? It's no one's business but ours." He checked his wristwatch and then glanced back at her. "I can have someone else keep an eye on Thistle for an hour or so to give you time to wash up and get something to eat. It's going to be a long night and Len told me you were here at dawn."

"Are you sure?" Frankie peered back into the stall where the horse paced. "I don't want to miss anything."

This was the whole reason she'd become a ranch hand. Not to fix drainage ditches or mend fences, although she'd understood that was part of the job description. She'd always been in it for the chance to work with animals.

"She's a first-timer. We've got a lot of hours before she foals."

"In that case, I'll be back in an hour or less. And thank you for giving me the chance to be here." She felt a pinch of guilt that he'd only extended the opportunity to her because he'd overheard her mentioning her need for hours in the barn to other ranchers at the gala.

Had she taken unfair advantage of their date?

"You've more than earned it," he told her easily, not sounding at all taken advantage of as he stepped closer to her. "But I'll give you fair warning that it's not just because I want to help you get into veterinary school that I'm inviting you back here tonight."

Something about the look in his eyes made her throat dry up. Gave her visions of the two of them twined around each other, peeling clothes off while they kissed. Touched. And more.

"You have an ulterior motive?" She shook off her imaginings, reminding herself she was still on the clock.

"I do." He leaned against the wooden framing of a vacant horse stall, his head inclined toward hers. "Because you might run from me, but I know you won't leave Thistle's side tonight. And I'm going to use that time to get to know you better, Frankie. Without the distraction of—" his gaze roamed over her in a way that set her on fire "—everything that distracted us last night."

"Then I'll consider myself warned." She tried for what she hoped was a playful tone, needing to keep things light.

With another man, she might be flattered. But Xander wasn't the type of guy who invested in romantic relationships. She'd been here long enough to take note of that. And she couldn't afford to get attached. Didn't dare give him a piece of herself that she wouldn't be able to get back when he walked away.

Xander's whole world had been tilted sideways since he'd woken up alone this morning, Frankie's peaches and roses scent still lingering in his sheets.

Now, as the clock neared midnight and Thistle's labor progressed in the birthing stall, he had to admit Frankie was still keeping him off-kilter. She was obviously excited to be in the barn for the delivery, a fact made evident by how many times she hopped up from the portable camp chair he'd moved into the barn for the night. They could both see into the stall from where he'd set up the chairs, a couple of yards away from the foaling area to help Thistle relax as much as possible. The mare's tail was wrapped and the foaling kit was handy.

Yet Frankie got out of her seat time after time to take a closer look, especially when the mare's back was to them or when she lay down in the straw.

"You must have assisted at plenty of animal births by now, I'll bet," he said, honest about wanting to get to know her better.

Tipping back in his chair, he watched as she settled in beside him again, the scent of hay and horses heavy in the air while fans moved some of the night air through the building.

"I have. I've been shadowing Doc Macallan for almost two years." She referenced a rural animal practice about ten miles west of Currin Ranch.

"He fills in here sometimes when our regular vet is away." Xander remembered him from when he was a kid; the guy was older than his dad.

"He helped me get hired on here, actually, so I could have a paying job that was close to his practice." She tightened the band around her ponytail, the crescent moon birthmark on her neck visible as she moved. "And he tries to schedule fieldwork on the days I'm around to shadow him, so I've gotten some cool experiences that way—from treating small wounds to emergency surgeries."

"And that's how you spend your days off from the ranch?"

"Most of them. Sometimes I squeeze in some time volunteering at an animal shelter, too. Because even though Doc Macallan has enough work to keep me busy, it can help my application to have multiple animal experiences."

"That's ambitious." He'd gotten his MBA in a condensed amount of time, but he hadn't needed to worry about the cost of the degree. "Will you be able to focus full time on your studies if you get accepted?"

"*When* I get accepted," she said immediately. Then she bit her lip and looked embarrassed. "Sorry. Positive thinking about that is a habit of mine, but I absolutely didn't mean to put words in your mouth."

He chuckled. "It's fine. Good for you."

"But to answer your question, I don't think I could manage the course load and working full time, too, so I'd definitely have to scale back my hours."

He asked her more about the animals she liked working with—dogs and horses were some of her favorites—and those that presented the biggest challenges. Cats could be fractious, she admitted, but apparently her vet had a recovering ostrich at his small farm and the bird had been a bit of a terror.

But what threw Xander was her caginess about her family and friends. She would discuss animals and her dreams for as long as he wanted, but she didn't seem inclined to share any more about her unusual upbringing or the fact that she'd left home at eighteen and hadn't looked back. He hadn't pushed, but he wondered how tough it must be for her to be without a family.

He mulled that over while she got up to check on Thistle for the fifth time in the last half hour. She was nothing if not devoted to the dam.

"Oh!" she called out softly from where she stood at the entrance to the birthing stall, her green eyes bright. "Xander, it's time. I see the hooves."

He bolted from his seat, cursing himself for not focusing on the mare. Thistle was lying down, and appeared as comfortable as a first-time mother could be during strong contractions. She was agitated and sweating, but she didn't seem to be fighting the labor. The mare blew hard.

"We'll monitor her over the next half hour." He wouldn't interfere unless Thistle stopped making progress.

The horse whinnied and tossed her head, nudging her side with her nose. The next contraction broke the water sac, and Frankie brought fresh straw while Xander kept his eye on the mother.

Half an hour later, a perfect black foal emerged.

It was a nice moment to share with Frankie, and they worked in tandem to clean up the stall and give the new mother room to recover. Once Thistle was on her feet again, they left the stall, taking turns washing up in the utility sink. Then, finally, they had time to watch the foal.

"She's so beautiful!" Frankie exclaimed as she returned to the bars of the stall, her voice full of awe. She reached for his arm and squeezed, as if to share her excitement. "Isn't she most precious thing?"

Her touch reminded him how amazing their night together had been. How much he wanted to be with her again. He wrapped an arm around her waist, holding her close to his side while they watched the baby's attempts to stand.

"She's a beauty, no doubt." His gaze slid to Frankie's profile while she watched the foal navigate her wobbly legs. "Let's give them some room to bond."

Her dark hair was in a ponytail, the end draped over her bare shoulder since she wore a black tank top that said Keep Calm and Cowgirl On.

"Of course." She nodded, misty-eyed as

she turned toward him. "We don't want Thistle to reject her own baby."

Something about the way she said it—a hint of wryness creeping into her tone—let him know she was thinking about something else. Her own parents? The night he'd driven her home from the rodeo she'd told him that her adoptive family found her wandering a road outside Laredo.

"It's very rare for that to happen." Xander rubbed her shoulder as they turned to sit in the seats outside the stall.

He flipped off a spotlight in the birthing stall now that the dam had safely delivered her foal. They could still see the animals in the glow of a lower-wattage lantern hanging overhead.

"Among horses, maybe." She dropped into the canvas folding chair and crossed one denim-clad leg over the other. "Humans are another story."

He reached over to take her hand, thinking how very different it was to sit beside her in a barn tonight after dancing her around a gala the evening before. At the gala, he'd been pursuing her, no question. Tonight, he saw her pain and couldn't help but feel protective.

"Do you have any reason to believe your birth parents abandoned you?" he asked gently.

"No. But I have no reason to believe they wanted me, either." She lifted her shoulder, as if to shrug it off, and the gesture looked as pained as the words sounded. "Who lets their two-year-old wander the streets?"

He could see her point. He stroked his thumb along the backs of her knuckles, wishing he could soothe away the hurt she felt. "I told you that my sister Maya was adopted, and I really do think my father's never told her—or any of us—how she came to be in our family because in his mind, he's protecting her in some way."

"Where is she now? I'm just surprised I've never seen her in all the time I've worked here." She peered over at him briefly before turning back to watch the foal nose around the stall in search of her dam.

"Maya has been away at college. She was supposed to come home this summer but she hasn't shown up yet. I'm hoping we'll see her soon, though. I miss her."

He'd ask Annabel if she'd heard from her. It seemed strange that she hadn't flown home for the summer yet.

"I don't know if I buy into the whole idea of protecting a child after she's reached adulthood. Whatever the truth is, it has to be better than not knowing," she told him with a fierceness in her voice, emotion in her gaze that was visible even in the dim lighting. "You can't properly process sorrow unless you understand it in the first place."

The mare nickered at her foal, encouraging her. Xander watched the baby try again to get on her feet while Frankie's words chased around his head.

"I'm not sure there's a right or wrong way to process sorrow." The words surprised him. He hadn't meant to share anything about Rena.

As much as he wished he could call them back, however, he knew that Frankie deserved to know the truth about him. About his own sense of loss.

She shifted to face him, her green eyes full of empathy as her fingers flexed around his hand. "I'm sorry, Xander. You lost your mother when you were young—"

"I did." He nodded, remembering those dark years when Annabel's mother had died and then his own mother passed away three years later. His father had barely finished grieving for his wife when Xander came to live with them. "I was fifteen when she died. But I was thinking of my fiancée."

She blinked. Twice.

"I'm so very sorry." She shook her head, her ponytail sweeping back and forth against her arm. "I didn't know you'd been engaged."

He nodded. "For six months. We were two months away from our wedding date when she died in a riding accident."

Even two years after the fact, the words still felt strange to say. Wooden and awkward. He'd never shared anything about Rena with any other woman he'd dated. He wasn't sure why it had come tumbling out tonight, but with an ache opening up in his chest, he realized now he wasn't ready to share any more about his convoluted relationship with Rena before her death.

"That must have been devastating." Frankie bit her lip. "I didn't mean to sound insensitive about grieving when I said what I did about sorrow—"

"You could never sound insensitive." He squeezed her hand, understanding all at once that the ache in his chest was only going to go away once he had Frankie with him again. He needed her tonight. "I only told you because I wanted you to…" To understand that he could never be that kind of man again? That he didn't have the emotional resources to be in a relationship like that again? "To know," he finished lamely.

He'd shared as much as he could about that.

The deeper hurt of his past with his fiancée wasn't something he was willing to trot out tonight.

Inside the birthing stall, Thistle's foal found her mother's udder and began to nurse. His work here for the night was done. Frankie's lips curved in a small smile at the sight, a happy note in a conversation that had hit too close to home.

"Thistle's a good mama," Frankie observed deftly, turning the topic away from Rena. "I'm glad I got to be with you tonight for this."

He knew she was talking about more than the delivery. And he was so damned grateful she hadn't pressed to learn more about his past. The relationship that had gutted him.

"I am, too," he admitted, needing her in his arms as fast as possible. To forget everything else but her. He tugged her to her feet, pulling her close, all the emotions beneath the surface finding the most appealing outlet. "And I'll walk you back to your cabin, no expectations, if you're ready for the night to end."

He didn't want to hurt her. She deserved better than what he could offer her.

"What's the alternative?" she asked breathlessly, her green eyes searching his. "Say, for example, I have some expectations about what happens afterward?"

An answering hunger surged. His fingers flexed on her hips as he restrained himself from kissing her here. Now.

"In that case, I come home with you, and I don't leave until the sun comes up."

Seven

Unlocking the door to her cabin half an hour later, Frankie knew she took a dangerous risk with her heart.

Xander's sorrow for his fiancée was tangible; she understood that now. She also recognized that he'd buried it in meaningless relationships. It hurt to know she was just another way to forget about the woman he'd loved.

And yet, as he followed her inside the cabin, Frankie's heart whispered that maybe she was different from his other affairs.

Hadn't he confided in her something significant tonight? Hadn't he told her he was disappointed when he woke up alone this morning?

What if there was a chance that they could have something more? She understood that he wanted to lose himself in their sizzling chemistry for the night. And since she needed that, too, she couldn't deny them both. As long as she remembered that this was only temporary, she would be okay.

She couldn't let herself forget that Xander had been clear about not wanting more.

Now, full of emotions from all they'd shared tonight, she hung her keys on a metal hook by the front door and turned into Xander. He was right there, a foot behind her, bolting the door behind them. He didn't hesitate. Twining his arms around her waist, he drew her more fully against him.

The scent of hay and antibacterial soap rose from their clothes, the warmth of his body intensifying the last hint of spicy aftershave under his neck as she rose on her toes to kiss him there. Her eyes drifted closed, the feel of him somehow already familiar, but different and exciting at the same time. She tunneled her fingers into his short hair, tilting his mouth down over hers.

The kiss fired through all her nerve endings, desire spiraling out from that point of contact. Xander's hands splayed along her back, pressing her to him tighter. Her breasts molded to the wall of muscle that was his chest, the feel of him making her knees weak, her limbs liquid. She made tiny, hungry sounds in the back of her throat as she tried tugging his T-shirt up and off, getting hung up on his wide shoulders until he helped her.

For a moment, she took in the sight of him, bare-chested and breathtaking, still just a step over the threshold of the cabin. The dim light from a nearby lamp burnished his skin with a golden glow.

"Come upstairs." Taking his hand, she pulled him with her to the steps that led to the loft of her small cabin, the area she'd made into her bedroom.

The smooth-planed log stairs led them up over the kitchen to the nook where she'd tucked a full-size bed and a nightstand. There wasn't room for much else. The scent of pine hung heavy in the air, even with the overhead fan spinning on low.

It was a far cry from the luxurious pool house where he'd taken her the night before. But they stood under the skylight, the white glow of the moon spilling over them. She'd always liked looking up at the stars before she fell asleep at night.

Reaching to pull Xander toward the bed, she noticed him frowning down at the living room from his stance near the heavy wood banister.

"We have bigger cabins around the ranch that are sitting vacant," he told her as he turned to face her. "I'll find you one with more room."

The different worlds that divided them felt very far apart.

"I'm happy here. It's more than I need." Living rent-free had helped nudge her closer to her goal of being able to pay for veterinary school.

"You should have a bedroom with four walls." He looped his arms around her neck, tipping his forehead to hers. "I'll make sure of it."

"I don't need help," she bristled, tensing. "I prefer to take responsibility for myself."

His jaw flexed. She could see the shift of shadows on his face, despite the dim lighting. He remained silent.

"Besides," she continued, needing to be very clear about this, "upgrading my accommodations on-site is the surest way to get everyone gossiping about us. People will say I'm getting preferential treatment, and that wouldn't be fair."

Waiting for his answer almost killed her. She didn't want to argue. Didn't want to think about all the things that divided them. They were better when they were working together—whether it was to deliver a foal or to make small talk with local ranchers like they did at the gala.

Xander nodded, some of the tension leaving his shoulders.

"All right. We'll leave it for now," he conceded, stroking a stray hair from her temple and smoothing it back as they stepped away from the banister and closer to the bed. "I just want you to be comfortable. Happy."

His touch stirred her, the heat that had been simmering earlier returning quickly. He bent to drop a kiss on her jaw, nibbling his way down her neck in a way that made quivers race up and down her spine. His hands slid beneath the hem of her tank, skimming up her ribs to stroke the undersides of her breasts through the lace of her bra. Desire unfurled and she sucked in a gasp.

"*This* makes me happy," she murmured, arching closer. "Your touch."

He studied her through heavy-lidded eyes, his thumbs stroking back and forth over the taut peaks pebbling against his hand. "In that case, I'll make sure to provide all the touching you want."

His voice smoked over her, the promise teasing a shiver from her as they stood together in the white spill of moonlight. Her calves nudged the footboard of her bed as she shifted on her feet.

"I'd like that." She ran her hands over his shoulders, his skin hot to the touch, the muscles shifting and tensing under her hands, his sensitivity as heightened as her own. "But getting naked will make all this more fun."

"Is that so?" He lowered one hand to flick open the button on her jeans, his fingers lingering in the square inch of skin he'd uncovered. "It could be rewarding to take our time."

Pleasure vibrated through her, the heady buzz of it thrumming along her nerve endings.

"No," she told him firmly, pressing her hips closer, her belly resting against the hard ridge behind his fly. "The best reward is putting an end to this hunger fast. To take the edge off. Afterward, we can discuss the merits of teasing touches."

"No one said anything about teasing," he clarified as he peeled her tank top up and off. His gaze roamed over her. "You're so damned beautiful."

His words moved her, especially since she knew she was a wreck after their work in the stables. She didn't have a chance to reply, however, as Xander moved to free the clasp on her bra and tug down the zipper on her jeans. The promise of being naked with him distracted her from everything else. Wriggling her way out of her clothes, she stripped off the rest of her garments while he discarded his denim and boots.

He flipped a foil packet on the pillow before drawing her onto the mattress with him in a tangle of limbs. She slid her arms around his neck, absorbing the sensation of having him next to her. The bristle of his jaw and the texture of the hair on his chest. The impressive muscle underneath it. His lean hips pinning hers while he stroked his way up her thigh.

Their gazes collided and she melted inside at the intensity of his expression. The heat in his gaze. She hooked her calf around his, wanting more. He shifted, his knee pressing hers wider. Her pulse raced.

When he kissed his way down her body, her breath caught. Each twitch of his lips turned her to liquid. She thought she might die of pleasure when, at last, he kissed her intimately. Her senses swam. She gripped the duvet beneath her, a fistful in each hand, as she braced herself for the completion shimmering so very close now.

Then it hit her and she cried out, the rush of fulfillment so strong that it broke over her again and again. Xander coaxed every last spasm from her before he stretched out above her, covering her. He retrieved the condom and rolled it into place while she tried to find her breath again.

She skimmed her hands over his arms and his chest, finally clutching his shoulders while he edged his way inside her. When they were fully joined, she kissed him deeply, her emotions winding around him along with her arms.

She wanted this moment to last, relishing the feel of him inside her, the tension threading through his muscles as he moved, the way the moonlight played off his skin, casting them in alternating shadows as they moved together in sync. Each thrust stoked the passion higher. Hotter.

He stole her breath away.

And possibly her heart.

She couldn't gather either of them as the fluttering sensation started in her womb. By the time it burst through her in another delicious spasm, she held him tight.

His shout resonated through her body along with the lush sensations. Once her senses returned and she became aware of her own breathing again, she knew something momentous had happened. Maybe not for Xander. But for her.

She'd known it was a risk to be with him

like this again, but she hadn't realized how quickly she might lose her heart to him. With tenderness welling up in her chest, she feared that was exactly what was happening. She was developing feelings for Xander Currin, a man who refused to fall for anyone since his true love had died.

But then, maybe that shouldn't come as a surprise when she'd swooned over him for months. Was it any wonder that this kind of time with him would make her want him in her life for more than just one night?

Breathe.

Just breathe.

Frankie staved off the chance of hyperventilating, knowing that wouldn't be a good way to end their night together. Instead, she kissed his bare shoulder and hoped for the best.

"Stay," she whispered in his ear, not ready for a conversation that might reveal some of what she was feeling. "Sleep."

She tugged the tangled duvet from where

it lay half on the floor, covering their cooling bodies.

Xander kissed her forehead, stroking aside her tumbleweed hair.

"Good night, Frankie." He tucked her against him, her ear pressed to the steady thrum of his heart.

She wondered, right before she fell asleep, was he truly saying good-night?

Or had he really meant goodbye?

Xander had every intention of spending what little remained of the night with Frankie. She didn't need to work in the morning since she'd spent long hours in the barns while the rest of the ranch slept. He'd thought he would make her breakfast, show her that she didn't need to worry about morning-after awkwardness between them. He felt certain they could just enjoy what was happening between them without having to look at more than one day at a time.

But his father had texted him in the pre-dawn hours to ask a question about Thistle, the message leading Xander to believe Ryder was wandering around the barns by himself. That alone would have been rare enough. Combined with the fact that he'd reached out to his son, and Xander knew something must be wrong. His father might ask Xander for help with the oil business, but he never inquired much about the ranch. Did his father find the same solace in the barns that Xander did? Concern about his dad was the only reason he left Frankie's side before the sun rose. It didn't have a damned thing to do with the heightened intimacy of their night together.

Dressing quietly so as not to wake her, he jammed his phone in his back pocket and left the cabin, heading toward the barns. It was a short walk, and he couldn't help but think there had to be better accommodations for her on the ranch. He respected her grit and her work ethic for taking on the ranch hand job in the first place, but she'd been on the team for almost a year so she deserved some consideration for her contributions. There were vacant cabins farther from the barns, with more room, but maybe she appreciated the proximity for the extra hours she put in.

He entered the horse barn in the gray light of predawn and found his father sprawled in one of the camp chairs outside the birthing stall.

"Xander." His father speared his fingers through his hair. "I didn't expect you to come down here at this hour."

He sounded surprised.

"And I didn't expect to hear from you," Xander returned, stroking the nose of his favorite work horse as he lingered by her stall. "You don't usually take a personal interest in the livestock."

His father had worked out of an office for years, more focused on oil than cattle.

"I needed to think about something else for a few days." Ryder tipped back in the chair, his boots crossed on the hay-strewn floor in front of him. "I figured I'd check on Thistle."

"She did well, and the foal nursed soon afterward. I told Len to check on them when he gets in." Still stroking Domino's nose, Xander didn't see a need to mention Frankie, not ready to share whatever was happening between them with anyone else.

Just taking her to the gala had been more of a commitment than he'd made to any woman in the last year. Certainly, it was a more public statement than he'd made about anyone else. He guessed she wouldn't be impressed if he told her that, however.

"The last couple of days have been... frustrating, to say the least." Ryder shrugged, his wrinkled tee suggesting he'd never gone to sleep the night before. "It's not every day that a woman walks out on me in public."

Angela Perry, Xander realized. He'd shoved the incident at the Flood Relief Gala to the back of his mind, but it was clear his father hadn't. "Have you spoken to her since she left the gala with Sterling?"

"She hasn't answered my calls or texts." His father leaned forward again, leaving the camp chair to pace the barn between stalls. The horses, picking up on his restlessness, stamped their hooves or tossed their heads. Ryder didn't seem to notice, though, a dark scowl etched in his features. The hint of frustration was unusual for him, since he was far more even-keeled than his longtime enemy, Sterling Perry.

"Her father has a lot of leverage over her," Xander pointed out, hoping to calm him down. "Not just because she holds the VP job with Perry Holdings. The emotional aspect has to weigh on her, too. Her dad was furious."

"He's always been a hothead. With too much damned pride." Ryder quit pacing to lean against a stall, frowning.

Xander didn't say anything, hoping his father might reveal something about his long enmity with Sterling. Had Ryder made overtures toward Sterling's young wife long ago?

But his father pulled his Stetson off a hook near the tack room and set it on his head.

"I should go see Angela in person," he announced, striding toward the exit.

"The sun isn't even up yet." Xander walked outside with him, breathing in the June air that was marginally cooler at this hour. "Are you sure that's wise?"

"Son..." His father stopped, his voice even more gravelly than normal from lack of sleep. "If I've learned one thing about relationships over the years, it's that you don't wait for them to fall apart before you pull your head out of the sand."

Did that mean a man should run headlong into trouble because a woman retreated for a day or two? Perhaps his skepticism showed in his expression, because his father shook his head.

"When it comes to relationship problems, a man's natural inclination might be to wait and hope things get better. But the women I've known tend to view that as a lack of caring." His father straightened, pulling his truck keys from his pocket. "So if a woman is unhappy with you, you're better off facing it head-on than finding out afterward that you lost out on something that could have been special."

Xander mulled that over while the first hints of purple lit the sky in the east. Would Frankie be unhappy with him that he'd left her side? Or would she be relieved that he hadn't made it awkward for her, something she'd been worried about after their first night together? He honestly didn't know.

"I still say she's not going to be thrilled when you knock on her door at dawn."

"Maybe not." Ryder tossed his Stetson on the passenger seat before he slid behind the wheel. "But I guarantee you she'll be glad I cared enough to show up. To try."

With that, he fired up the engine and took off in a plume of dust, taillights glowing red.

Xander stood in front of the horse barn, halfway between the main ranch house and Frankie's cabin. The pull of her was so damned strong. He wanted to be with her again. And again. He also wanted to help her get into vet school. Move her into a more comfortable cabin. Keep introducing her to prominent members of the Texas Cattleman's Club so she had a ready clientele for her practice.

But he knew in his heart that she deserved more than that. She had focused all her love and affection on animals as a kid because her parents hadn't given her any other viable outlets for friends. Didn't that say something about her? She'd resented them enough to leave home at eighteen and not look back, so chances were good she was a tough judge of character when someone didn't live up to her expectations.

Hell yes, she deserved better than what Xander had to give.

In theory, he *could* go back to her place right now, and maybe she'd never be the wiser that he left. After all, his father certainly had a point that it carried weight in a relationship to show up and make that effort.

But as much as Xander wanted Frankie, he still couldn't risk the heartbreak that came with a relationship.

Not now. Not ever.

He pivoted toward the main house and headed home.

Ryder arrived at Angela's downtown condo after sunrise, the pink-and-orange sky warming the limestone building with the same colors. He parked his truck and took the elevator up to the fifteenth floor after giving his name to the security guard.

He hadn't warned her he was on the way. No sense giving her a chance to bail. At least she hadn't refused to see him.

Knocking on her door, he waited for her to answer. A moment later the door swung wide, and Angela greeted him in a fitted navy blue dress with silver buttons up the front. Her hair was still damp from her shower, her face free of any makeup. She looked beautiful, and he wished like hell their evening together had ended differently two nights ago.

The scent of her soap mingled with fragrant coffee brewing from somewhere in her apartment.

"Ryder." She hesitated only a moment before stepping back and opening the door wide for him. "Come in."

"I know it's early." He stepped inside, wondering if he should have brought something. Flowers, maybe. "But I really wanted to see you."

He'd never visited her apartment before, but she'd been easy enough to find. She'd referenced her downtown apartment building when she'd been discussing local real estate before she closed the deal for the Houston property that had become the location for the new Texas Cattleman's Club. He recalled her saying that her twin sister, Melinda, lived in the same condominiums.

"It's fine." Angela closed the door behind him and waved him toward the kitchen. "Can I get you some coffee?"

"Sure. Thank you." He followed her into the open-concept kitchen and living area, where the expansive views of downtown were visible from the huge windows out to the terrace.

"I was going to call you today anyhow." Barefoot, she padded silently over the hardwood floors to take a second mug from a cupboard. "I just needed a little time yesterday to sort through things in my mind."

He heard the stilted tone in her voice and knew it didn't bode well for them. Whatever she needed to "sort through" couldn't be good. He watched as she poured him a cup of coffee from the elaborate stainless steel machine before topping off her own. She slid the mug and a spoon across the counter toward him as he settled into a spot at the breakfast bar.

"I'm sorry that you were put in an awkward position at the gala." He peered around her living space, which was as tastefully appointed and restrained as the woman herself.

The gray couches and white accents were broken up by an occasional splash of yellow. There weren't many photos anywhere, but one silver framed picture held an image of her and Melinda flanking their father.

Another one—from when she was much younger—showed her and her youngest sister, Esme, with their mother, Tamara. Memories swamped him. Tamara Perry had been a rich man's daughter who married for duty and power but wanted love. Her husband had always paid more attention to business than his wife, and Ryder had always thought that was damned foolish of Sterling. Of course, Ryder had made the same mistake with his first wife, Penny, and regretted it.

All the more reason to ensure he didn't make those kinds of mistakes again. He refocused his attention back on Angela, where it belonged.

"Are you?" she asked him, passing the sugar bowl his way before he waved it off. "Sorry, that is? I wondered afterward if your invitation to the gala was just another way to continue your rivalry with my father. Maybe it was the perfect opportunity to get under his skin?"

The suggestion rankled.

"Absolutely not." He waited until she sat beside him at the breakfast bar, giving her 100 percent of his focus. "Angela, I tried like hell to ignore this attraction because I knew it would make things difficult for you."

"Until I kissed you." Her expression softened at the memory of that shared kiss. "I surprised myself that day."

"You surprised me, too, but I'm glad you did." He wanted to take her hand. To touch her, and convince her that he didn't have anything but good intentions where she was concerned. But this conversation was too important for them to get sidetracked by attraction. "I couldn't exactly pretend I didn't feel something for you once that kiss happened."

A sad smile curved her lips before she took a sip of her coffee from a bright red cup that said "girl boss" in white script. His mug, on the other hand, was plain white. He'd bet hers had been a gift.

"The real question is are *you* sorry that we kissed?" Ryder continued, watching her pretty profile while she sipped her drink. "Is the pressure from your father too much? Are we going to throw in the towel on this already?"

He didn't realize how much he wanted to keep seeing her until he'd voiced the question. But now, with their fledgling relationship hanging in the balance, he knew that he wanted Angela in his life.

A memory of Xander's expression this morning crossed his mind, reminding Ryder how far away his son was from realizing that living without love was a lonely way to move through the world. Xander still thought he was protecting his heart by keeping the pretty ranch hand at arm's length. When really, he was only hurting himself. And her.

Damned foolish, but he couldn't tell Xander that in so many words or his son would only dig his heels in deeper.

Ryder didn't want that for him and Angela.

"I'm not sure." She set her mug on the granite counter and swiveled toward him on the leather padded bar stool. "I spent yesterday at Perry Ranch, and I spoke to one of the maids who remembered you from the time you worked there. She made it sound like there might have been more to your relationship with my mother than just friendship."

The hurt in her voice cut right through him. How could they be back to this? He'd thought those blasted rumors had finally died when Tamara passed, but apparently someone was giving the story new life. He clenched his fist, wishing he could make those ugly accusations disappear.

"Angela." This time, he did touch her, covering her hand with his. "I cared deeply for your mother, but I never had romantic feelings toward her." He'd never worried about what the rest of the world thought about his relationship with Tamara, but he damned well cared what Angela thought. "I swear to you, I never so much as kissed her, let alone anything more."

She was quiet so long he feared he'd already lost her faith in him. But then she gave a small nod.

"Thank you for sharing that. I—" She closed her eyes for a moment and then opened them again. "I have a lot to think about."

Disappointment landed heavy on his shoulders. Sliding his hand away from hers, he told himself not to push her. He didn't blame her for being confused. Her father had hated him all her life, so it had come as a surprise that she'd even considered being with him in the first place.

Maybe he just needed to give her time.

"We shared a beautiful friendship," he said finally, wanting to put what he'd had with Tamara into some kind of context for her. "A friendship that your grandfather recognized. That's the only reason he gave me that land. Because I'd been a friend to your mother when she needed one."

There wasn't anything more to say about that. Angela would have to either believe him or not, because there wasn't a soul on earth who knew what had happened between him and Tamara the few times they were alone besides Tamara and him. And her mother had died in a car accident the same year that Xander had lost his mother.

Three years after Ryder had lost Elinah.

The hits had kept coming during those years. Losing Elinah had devastated him, so Ryder could understand why it was tough for Xander now, when his son was learning to move on without the woman he'd planned to marry. Xander had all but retreated from the world after Rena died, immersing himself in the foreman job at Currin Ranch, the only work he'd cared about. And Ryder had understood the pain all too well, which was why he'd allowed Xander to stay in a job that didn't utilize his brilliant business mind. He believed his son would come around one day and want to learn the business. To embrace the CEO job at Currin Oil.

The toughest truth Ryder had ever faced was that life continued to go on, even after the people he loved most in the world had died.

The loss of Elinah had almost killed him.

But here he was, putting one foot in front of the other. Trying to find happiness. And the woman next to him was the best chance he'd had since then.

Beautiful Angela Perry, his enemy's daughter.

But Ryder wasn't willing to let rumors and old gossip cost him this shot at something deeper with this rare and lovely woman who still looked at him like he meant something. Like he could make her happy. If there was even the slightest chance that he could find love again with Angela, he was sure as hell going to try.

Eight

In the morning, after a quick stop in the barn to check on Thistle and the new foal, Frankie tried to decide how to spend her unexpected time off. She lingered with the horses, scratching one of the older mares on the muzzle, wondering if she should take her out for a ride as a way to ease the ache in her chest that felt dangerously close to heartbreak.

Waking up alone this morning, when she'd been fully expecting to see Xander in bed beside her, had hurt. Hours later, she still couldn't shake the sense that the night to-gether that had been so significant to her hadn't meant anything to him.

She'd known better than to let herself get attached to a man who never stayed with one woman for long. She was supposed to be in it strictly for fun. For the toe-curling kisses, the off-the-charts sex, the physical release that was so good it was practically transcendent.

Except her emotions couldn't seem to re-sist getting involved, no matter how many times she reviewed the ground rules.

Stepping out of the barn, she decided to walk instead of ride this afternoon. There was a shady path around one of the irriga-tion ponds that would keep her out of the sun. Normally, she spent all her downtime volunteering with the animal shelter or shad-owing Doc Macallan on his rounds. And she loved that work. But today, she was glad to have a few hours to herself to get her head on straight.

She hurried her pace as she passed the

main house, but she stopped when she heard a woman's raised voice.

"Frankie!"

Annabel Currin waved to her from the driveway near the side yard where she walked from the garage with her keys in her hand.

"Hello," Frankie called, returning the wave and hoping Xander wasn't around.

She wasn't ready to see him yet.

Already, Annabel was hurrying toward her, tucking her keys in a yellow leather handbag as she went. She wore a white sundress with a bright turquoise necklace. Beaded blue-and-yellow sandals glinted in the bright sun. No surprise the style blogger looked beautiful and fashionable.

"Do you have a minute? I've got lunch waiting for me in the pool house, and I'm sure there's plenty for two." She gestured toward the building where Xander had taken Frankie after the gala. "There's an outdoor table under the overhang, so it's cool enough to sit there and still feel like we're getting a little fresh air."

A landscaping service truck was just pulling out of the driveway. The scent of freshly cut grass hung in the air, all the flowers and trees manicured to perfection.

Frankie hesitated, mostly because she didn't want to run into Xander when she hadn't figured out a game plan yet. "That's kind of you, but I was just heading to the pond for a walk."

"You'll melt in this heat," Annabel declared, gesturing toward the pool area. "Sit with me for a few minutes so I can at least get the scoop on how things went at the gala."

Annabel was too warmhearted to deny. Besides that, it felt nice to have someone *want* to spend time with her. As an only child, with parents who'd kept her isolated, Frankie really hadn't made friends until she'd left home. Even then, she'd moved around so much, trying to find a place that felt "right," she hadn't grown close to many people.

"If you're sure." She might as well enjoy

the fact that she didn't have any plans for the day. "But you don't need to feed me."

"Trust me, there will be plenty. Our cook still prepares food for me like I'm getting ready for a growth spurt." Annabel laughed as she opened the gate to let them inside the pool area. "I don't think she realizes I'm no longer twelve."

Frankie's gaze went straight to the pool house, memories of her night with Xander swamping her. The whole evening had been magical, from her Cinderella makeover and beautiful dress to the way Xander had made her feel.

She didn't realize she'd stopped on the deck to stare at the doors until Annabel said her name. From the puzzled expression on her friend's face, she guessed it wasn't the first time she'd called to her.

"Hmm? I'm sorry, I was thinking what a pretty spot this would be to read a book." Distractedly, she followed Annabel to the wrought iron patio table tucked under the pergola covered with vines and greenery.

A misting hose sprayed the finest cloud of cooling water while an overhead fan kept the temperature to a bearable level.

"I love coming out here to work on my blogs. But I want to know all about your evening at the gala. Did you have a good time?" Annabel dropped her purse into one of the patio chairs before tucking into a seat herself.

"It was amazing," she told her honestly, sliding into the chair opposite Annabel, already feeling cooler as they sat in the shade. "I'd never been to the Four Seasons, and I couldn't believe how stunning it looked with all the flowers."

She'd pressed the orchid Xander had given her between sheets of wax paper to preserve it. Not to overly romanticize him or the date. But her parents had been adamantly opposed to big populated venues, ensuring she hadn't gone to public school or experienced a prom night. So in a weird way, the Flood Relief Gala had been her first formal.

Maybe she had totally romanticized it.

But in an era where romance was dead, who could blame her for holding tight to a few girlish traditions?

"It was beautiful," Annabel agreed as she slid an extra plate and crisp linen napkin toward Frankie. Her smile faded. "We didn't stay for long, but we did make a brief appearance."

Something seemed off about that, making her wonder if Annabel had a falling-out with her fiancé.

"Is everything okay?" she asked, laying the napkin over her lap.

"Fine. It's fine." Annabel brushed aside the concern with an airy wave of her hand, her smile returning as she pulled off the cover on a chilled plate of finger sandwiches. Her diamond engagement ring still glittered on her hand. "So what did Xander think of your gala look?"

Frankie wondered about friend etiquette in a situation like that where she suspected something had upset Annabel. Would it help to talk about it? Then again, she didn't know Annabel all that well, so she hated to press her.

"He seemed to like it." Frankie couldn't help the smile that came with the memory of their first dance.

"I'll bet he did. That dress was fantastic on you." Annabel passed the plate of finger sandwiches toward her while she poured two glasses of water from a pewter pitcher.

"That's a ton of sandwiches," Frankie offered as an aside, taking one after all.

Although they were tiny—just a couple of bites each—they were piled in a neat stack of circles, each layer a little smaller than the last.

"I know," Annabel exclaimed, sliding two onto her own plate. "We could invite all our friends and still have enough. But back to your date." She slanted a more sidelong glance her way. "I feel like it must have gone well because I made a trip out to the barn last night to check on Thistle, and I heard both of your voices."

"You were there?" She tried to remember

what they'd talked about last night when they weren't focused on helping the mare.

Xander had asked her a lot about her plans for vet school, and the preparations she was making to be accepted into a program.

Things hadn't heated up until later.

"Just long enough to realize that Thistle was already well tended." She peered over her shoulder, as if checking to be sure they were alone. Then she leaned forward to confide, "And to be honest, it was nice to hear my brother sound…happy. So I decided not to interrupt."

"You don't think he's been happy these last months?" Surprised to hear Annabel's view of her brother, Frankie wondered if she'd missed the signs that Xander was still grieving his fiancée during the time she'd worked here.

"He puts on a good front, but he's not the same man he was before Rena's death."

It stung to realize she'd never really known the version of Xander that Annabel talked about. Perhaps some of the hurt showed on her face, because Annabel clapped a hand on her wrist.

"But you're good for him, Frankie. There was a tone in his voice last night that I haven't heard in a very long time."

Could that be true? Or was Annabel just hearing evidence that her brother was healing simply because she loved him and wanted to believe that?

"I'm not so sure." Setting aside the remainder of the egg salad sandwich she'd sampled, Frankie leaned back in her chair, tension balling in her stomach. "He left in the middle of the night without telling me. I thought we—" She forced herself to stop, to button down the notion that she had hoped they were growing closer. She was unaccustomed to sharing her personal life. "I just don't want you to get your hopes up, because I don't have any reason to believe we'll ever have another date."

She'd tried so hard to tell herself she was just having fun. But waking up alone had been far from it.

"That must have been hurtful." Annabel frowned, her eyes full of empathy. "I'm sorry he treated you that way, Frankie, but for what it's worth, he's loved in the past. I believe he can be persuaded to love again."

Frankie appreciated the thought. But she knew it was also heavily slanted toward what Annabel wanted to believe. Of course she hoped that Xander would find love again.

That didn't mean he was capable of giving his heart to someone. Rena was gone. And Frankie was just… Frankie.

She knew she wasn't anything like the women he normally dated.

"It's okay," Frankie reassured her, unwilling to accept any more of Annabel's kindness when she'd been convincing herself to stay away from Xander anyhow. "I knew when I accepted his offer to go with him to the Flood Relief Gala that he's…not looking for anything serious."

She pasted a smile on her face. Because she'd been fine with that. She'd even assured herself that she wanted that, too. To put an end to her distracting crush and get him out of her system before she went to veterinary school.

"What about you?" Annabel's dark eyes seemed to see straight through her. "Are you okay with that?"

She was terrified that she wouldn't be.

But she had no choice.

"Of course." She nodded, hearing the false note in her voice.

And knowing that Annabel couldn't miss it.

"Okaaay," Annabel said slowly enough to acknowledge that she wasn't buying it. "But Xander is a good man. And if it was up to me, you wouldn't give up on him yet."

Frankie nodded, unable to speak, let alone commit to what she suggested. But she enjoyed the other woman's friendship. The moment to share some of what she was going through.

Instead, she sipped her water, wishing it would cool the new emotion simmering inside her. Because the little flicker of hope she felt at Annabel's words was bound to burn her if she couldn't keep her emotions on lockdown.

Thankfully, Annabel steered their conversation toward lighter topics, topping off their drinks. Lemon, lime and orange wedges mixed with the ice.

"There's a Texas Cattleman's Club planning meeting next week, by the way." Annabel checked her phone as she spoke and then settled the device back on the table. "Even if you don't want to move forward with Xander romantically, you would benefit from getting to know the most influential ranchers in the area."

"A meeting?" Curious, she tried to shove aside her thoughts about Xander to focus on her career dream.

"It won't be as stuffy as it sounds. The TCC movers and shakers will all be there, so they're holding it in a conference suite at a local historic inn called the Haciendas. There will be a cocktail meet and greet afterward. I'm sure I can get you an invitation."

"Will you be there?" Frankie asked, thinking it would be more fun with Annabel in attendance. Besides, she'd need a barrier if Xander was there.

"Maybe." She checked her phone again, her brow furrowing as she squinted to see it despite the sunlight. "I've been messaging Maya to convince her to come home for the summer and attend some of the TCC events, but I haven't heard back from her yet."

"I'd like to meet her," Frankie murmured, remembering the story Xander had told her about Maya not knowing the identity of her birth parents. She definitely had that in common with Xander's adopted youngest sibling.

When they finished their visit a little while later, Frankie thanked her and tucked away the idea of asking Xander about the meet and greet after the TCC meeting. Checking with him about that sounded easier than Annabel's other suggestion—that she give romance a chance with Xander.

That sounded risky. Dicey.

And it had the potential to hurt her badly.

Yet in the past, she'd prided herself on never giving up without a fight. Not her dream of breaking free from her family's constraints. Not her hope of attending college. She'd even tried bronc riding.

Was she going to start running from a challenge now? Frankie ground her teeth together, not ready to be the kind of woman who turned tail and ran at the first bumpy patch in the road. Ever since she'd left home, she'd told herself she was going to embrace every possible new experience to make up for the suffocating world of her childhood.

Maybe she wasn't ready to give up on Xander yet.

Maya Currin stared at the fifth text from her sister, Annabel, and huffed a sigh.

She loved Annabel and missed her sister more than anyone else back home. But no matter how many sweet notes she got from her, Maya wasn't going back to Houston this summer.

No way. No how.

Stabbing the phone icon on her screen, she called her sister to tell her as much so she could move on with her day. Sitting by herself at a picnic table under the pine trees while four hundred tween-aged campers finished their lunches, Maya waited for Annabel to pick up.

"Maya!" Annabel squealed with the soft Texas drawl that Maya missed in this corner of the world. "Where in the world are you, and why haven't you come home yet? I haven't heard from you in ages."

"No guilt-tripping allowed," Maya snapped, more sharply than she'd intended. Then, softening her tone, she said, "I miss you too much already."

"Sorry, sweetie. Is everything okay? Are you still at school?"

Maya had just finished her freshman year at Boston College, but she was too mad at her father to return home this summer. Not that she needed to share that part with Annabel and drag her into that drama.

A few campers ran past her toward their

next activity, shoving each other and laughing, their footsteps pounding the packed dirt under the pines.

"Everything's fine. I just decided to take a summer job at a sleepaway camp on Cape Cod." She'd applied to as many jobs as she could think of to justify the time away from home.

She'd turned eighteen this year, and her father *still* hadn't told her the story of her birth and how he came to adopt her. Even though he'd promised. Why was he hiding the real story? What was he so afraid of her finding out?

"A job?" Annabel sounded deflated. "Do you get any time off? I wanted you to go to some of the fancy Texas Cattleman's Club events for the opening of the Houston chapter."

"Really?" She asked only because she was hungry for news of home. Even though she was mad at her dad. Even though she wouldn't go home until he told her the truth.

For now, she just missed Annabel. The

sleepaway camp was okay, but it wasn't home. She even missed the Houston heat, since Cape Cod was having a cool spell. She wore a hoodie in the middle of the day.

"Yes! It's the summer of galas and parties. I thought maybe you could be a guest on my blog and I could make you over."

It meant a lot to her that Annabel wanted to hang out. That she mattered to someone back home, even if her father thought she was still a kid who couldn't be trusted with the most basic information.

Like the name of her birth parents.

"That sounds fun," she admitted, her chest hurting while a long line of junior campers walked past with their counselor toward the archery field. "I'm sorry I can't be there. I'll be working all summer."

Annabel made idle chitchat a while longer, until Maya heard the bell that precipitated the next activity change.

"I'm sorry to cut you short, but I have to get back to the stables," she told her older sister as she hurried to her feet. "We'll catch up soon, okay?"

She disconnected fast, before the mixture of homesickness and anger at her father became apparent in her voice. No need to upset Annabel.

Maya would figure out how to get back at her father soon enough. For starters, she was certain it would get his attention if she didn't return to school in the fall.

He wouldn't be able to ignore her then.

Finishing up a few phone calls on the private flight home from Amarillo, Xander tipped his head back in the leather seat and wondered about his next call.

To Frankie.

He had missed her during this unexpected trip. He hadn't seen her for three days, since he'd been called away on Currin Ranch business with zero warning.

He didn't appreciate his father orchestrating the trip that had ended up being more executive-level than Xander had been led to believe. Attending stock sales was part of the job as foreman, but Ryder had asked him to meet with several ranch owners in Amarillo while he was there.

Was that his father's way of coercing Xander into taking a more active role in the business? By doubling up his work responsibilities?

With the TCC planning committee meeting just two days away, Xander knew tensions were ratcheting up in the group since Sterling and Ryder were locked in a power struggle. Whereas even a month ago he hadn't really cared about the new Texas Cattleman's Club branch, Xander found himself wanting more buy-in now. Was that because he was starting to put his grief to rest for good? Or was it because Frankie had taken an interest in the TCC and he wanted the group to be a warm, welcoming place for her?

Possibly a little of both.

Either way, he couldn't deny that knowing her had brought him back to life in a lot of ways. He hadn't completely balked at the

Amarillo venture, for one thing. And even though he hadn't appreciated not being consulted about the added meetings, he hadn't found them as tedious as he might have in the past months.

His brain was kicking back to life to the point where he wondered about the possibility of stepping into the role that awaited him at Currin Oil—the CEO position once his father stepped down.

Maybe he was even ready for more with Frankie. At the very least, he wanted to see her again. That in itself was a huge step forward for him.

Dialing her number, he stared out the plane's window as the flight neared Houston. The light on the wing blinked back at him in the dark.

"Hello?" Her voice, soft and sexy, triggered a wave of longing and lust.

Damn, but he'd missed her.

"It's Xander." He regretted not calling her before now, since he'd been the one to walk away last time. He'd messaged her that he was going out of town, but she hadn't replied. "I'm going to be back home in about an hour."

"You'll be pleased to know the ranch is still standing." Her voice struck him as carefully neutral.

He hoped that didn't mean she was upset with him. Because he'd been looking forward to seeing her all day. He hadn't expected to miss her as much as he had.

"I'm more interested in how you're doing." He gripped one of the armrests as the jet hit a pocket of turbulence. "I've missed you."

The silence on the other end lingered a beat too long.

"I assumed you'd moved on," she finally replied. "When I woke up without you, I figured maybe that was your way of letting me know things had cooled off."

He closed his eyes, regretting that he'd hurt her. She'd probably observed more of his bachelor ways than he'd realized over the last year.

"Not even close." Thinking about that night

together in her cabin revved him up even now. "I wanted to talk to you, but when my dad asked me to take the Amarillo trip for the stock sale, I couldn't say no. His plate's full with Texas Cattleman's Club responsibilities and the ongoing battle with Sterling."

"How'd the sale go?" she asked, drawing him into a conversation that lasted straight through the landing and well into his ride home.

She'd seemed interested in every aspect of the sale, from the business side to questions about the trends in breeds he was seeing. She knew a surprising amount about cattle, but she also had questions about the possibility of sheep and goats at Currin Ranch, ventures that had been discussed as ways to diversify and grow the business.

It wasn't until he steered the truck under the ranch's welcome sign that he realized how long they'd talked.

"How do you feel about company when I get home?" he asked, wanting to see her.

Touch her. Talk to her more.

"I'm not really dressed for company. Maybe tomorrow?"

Disappointment stung. Right up until a wicked laugh floated through the phone.

"Unless you don't mind seeing me in my nightclothes," she added, a sly note in her voice.

Desire for her surged and he tapped the gas harder.

"I'll be at your door in five minutes."

Nine

Xander wanted to romance her.

He'd missed her, and tonight, he planned to show her how much.

But when Frankie answered the door of her cabin in a sleep T-shirt and nothing else, any words he'd been going to say dried right up and vanished. With no makeup and her dark hair tousled, she robbed the rest of his reason when she slid her arms around his neck and kissed him.

She was warm and soft, every delectable nuance of her body apparent through the well-washed fabric of the tee. He coiled his arms around her waist and hoisted her against him. He toed the cabin door closed behind them with his boot and carried her deeper into the cabin, every step causing sweet friction, making him burn hotter. Harder.

Her lips were perfect, molding to his one moment, sliding down to the hollow of his throat the next. She was as hungry for this as he was, as restless for what they'd found the other times they'd been together.

When he started up the stairs to the loft, she locked her ankles around his waist, anchoring them together. Every step tantalized him, the movement eliciting a throaty moan from her in a way that only compounded the teeth-grinding need he felt.

Reaching the bed, he deposited her in the middle of the comforter, the scent of lavender and warm woman rising from the linens while he wrenched off his shirt and unfastened his belt. Her green eyes tracked his actions, lingering on his chest before dipping lower.

Without taking her gaze off him, she reached for a condom on the bed and shifted to her knees while he removed the last of his clothes.

"May I?" she asked.

"Hell, yes." He couldn't have been more eloquent, his whole world narrowed to the all-consuming need.

She tore open the package with zero finesse, but her hands were careful—oh, so damned careful—as she rolled the condom in place. He nearly didn't survive the process, especially when she stroked her hand from base to tip, as if to test her handiwork. The touch wrenched a groan from him, desire for her so intense it ached.

He skimmed off her T-shirt and tipped her back against the comforter, positioning himself over her. Locking eyes with her, he slid inside her, joining them. Her breasts pushed against his chest and he claimed her mouth, kissing her over and over, letting the heat build as he rocked his hips.

Her nails raked his back, her teeth sinking

into his shoulder. He appreciated the sting when he was so damned close to losing it. Forcing himself to slow down, he listened to her breathing, taking her where she needed to go.

She was close, too, and it wasn't long before her back arched hard, her release coming in one sweet wave after another. He didn't have a prayer of lasting after that, so he let himself follow her, the pleasure so perfect he couldn't remember ever feeling this close to anyone.

And this time, he wasn't going anywhere.

When their breathing finally slowed, he hauled her back against him to keep her close to him, making sure she knew how much he wanted her right there.

All night long.

Frankie slid from her bed before dawn.

Not to leave. Just to put on the coffee and revel in the most perfect night ever.

As the pink fingers of sunrise crept toward the horizon, she leaned on the kitchen countertop and stared out over the hayfields behind her cabin, thinking she could get used to this. She had succeeded in turning her crush on Xander into something more—something tangible—and it had led to the best sex of her life. She understood now why it had to be temporary. That Xander couldn't give more than this because he'd lost the love of his life.

The reality of it had settled in after her talk with Annabel, when she'd realized that she wasn't ready to give up whatever it was that they shared. Temporary or not, she wanted him in her life. And maybe—just maybe— it would be okay this way. Because Frankie had to focus on getting into vet school anyhow. There could still be a middle ground where they simply enjoyed the here and now without worrying about when it ended. Yet, as much as she reassured herself of that, something still felt...off about her thoughts. Maybe she was just overthinking things. They barely knew each other, after all.

Things had progressed so fast between

them, but she was only just beginning to get to know him.

The scent of coffee filled the kitchen, the sound of the machine percolating punctuated by a chime that let her know the brew was set.

"Good morning." Xander's voice was a welcome, deep hum across her senses as she straightened from the countertop.

Bare-chested and sporting a pair of half-buttoned jeans, he was absurdly handsome in her kitchen as he leaned a hip against the stove. His dark hair looked like a wild woman had raked her fingers through it over and over during the night.

Which, of course, she had.

"I must have been lost in thought." Pleasure smoked through her at the memory of how thoroughly she'd lost herself in being with him. "I didn't even hear you come down the stairs."

"You were probably too busy fantasizing about what we could be doing right now if you'd stayed in bed with me."

How could he turn her on so thoroughly when they'd just been together hours before? Her belly flipped at the idea of being with him again.

"Maybe I was." Happiness curled around her at having him here with her. She pulled mugs down from a cupboard. "Or maybe I was just surprised we made it through a night together with no one running out the door."

She didn't mean to break the mood, but that's exactly what her comment had done. She could see it in the way his smile faded.

"I regret leaving that night. I'm so sorry if I upset you." He slid onto one of the counter stools at the narrow breakfast bar that took the place of a table in her small cabin.

Carrying the two mugs over to him, she sat on the stool next to his. "I don't know why I brought that up—"

"It's fine. I knew my dad was wrestling with some problems that night and went outside to talk to him. I should have left you a note."

"Xander, I know you're not ready for anything more. I'm fine with that." She'd been bracing herself for him to walk away since that first night.

"I didn't leave because I wanted to break things off. But you deserve to know the truth about why I've been so hell-bent not to repeat what happened with Rena."

"Anyone would have been heartbroken to lose their fiancée," she assured him, her hand covering his forearm.

"She ended our engagement right before the accident."

Frankie's coffee cup froze on the way to her lips. Her gaze flew to Xander's. The stark truth of the words was reflected there.

"I've never told anyone," he continued, taking a sip from his steaming cup. "Not a single soul. We'd argued the night before she went on the trip with her girlfriends. I told her she was overreacting when she said she wanted to call off the wedding. That she was just having jitters and it would be fine when she got back home."

She slid her palm under his and squeezed it, not wanting to interrupt when the memory was clearly painful to him.

Setting his mug back on the white tile counter, he stared down at their clasped hands.

"After she'd fallen, when I drove like a madman to get there, hoping somehow I'd reach her bedside before she died, I was too upset to figure out whether her parents or her friends knew that she'd called it off." He shook his head before he peered up at her again. "I'm still not sure if they knew she was ready to start a new life without me."

"I'm so sorry." Frankie's heart ached for how much he'd had to grieve for at once. "That had to have made losing her all the more difficult and stressful. You had to deal with navigating what people did or didn't know, and at a time you were devastated and could have used their support."

"It's in the past. It took me some time, but I've moved on." He slid his hand from hers to take another sip from his mug.

To keep her at arm's length? Or because he needed more coffee? She told herself not to overthink things. To just be in the moment.

"I'm glad." She bit her lip, wondering if he really had moved on considering his refusal to be in a serious relationship. But that wasn't her business, since "serious" wasn't what they were about. "And I appreciate knowing what was going through your head that night when you took off."

Xander's phone vibrated, but he ignored it, focused on her.

"It took me some time to put Rena in the past because I wasn't just dealing with losing her. I was trying to figure out how I could have missed the signs that she wanted out." He rolled his shoulders, as if shrugging away a weight.

"Did she say why?"

"Not anything that made sense to me. She said something about needing more time to find ourselves. As if I didn't know exactly who I am and what matters to me already." His jaw flexed just remembering the conversation. "But I don't think that was the real reason. And I know she didn't just make a snap decision about it. It was building for a while and I didn't see it. Or I did, but I chose to ignore it. Hell, I don't know."

She couldn't imagine how he'd worked through those things after her sudden death. No wonder it had taken him time to move on. While she searched for the right words to offer what comfort she could, he continued speaking.

"I immersed myself in work on the ranch for a long time, but this trip to Amarillo made me realize I'm ready to get back to my future with Currin Oil."

Surprised, she tried to imagine working here every day without seeing Xander. The vision of Currin Ranch without her favorite Currin left her feeling hollow. She barely fit into his world when she was a ranch hand and he was the foreman. How much greater would the divide be when he took over a multibillion-dollar corporation?

"Really? That's wonderful. Your father

must be thrilled." She tried to hide her mixed emotions, knowing she should be happy for him. Knowing it shouldn't matter. She had her own dreams she was excited to follow, after all, and he'd been supportive of them.

Yet their worlds would be so very different.

"I haven't told him yet. I only just figured it out last night on the flight home." He stroked a hand over her knee, his palm a warm weight even through the denim of her work clothes. "I also wanted to see if you'd attend the next Texas Cattleman's Club planning meeting with me. There's a meet and greet afterward and I could introduce you around."

Touched that she didn't even have to ask him about the party, she tried to focus on the positives. Xander might be leaving his work on the ranch, but at least he was still thinking of her. Helping her to achieve her dreams. Maybe that boded well for them to enjoy their affair a little while longer, until the flame burned out.

She wasn't sure what to think about his

revelation about Rena, let alone how it affected them. She needed time to think about that, too. At times like this, her lack of experience with people felt all the more frustrating. If she hadn't been raised in a vacuum, might she understand Xander better?

"Annabel mentioned the meet and greet. I'd be glad to go with you." That much, she was sure of.

"Then it's a date." He finished his coffee before standing. "I'll let you get to work and I'll tell Len you'll need the day off for the meeting. Can you be ready to leave by noon?"

"For sure." She put a lock on her runaway emotions, struggling to understand where she would fit in his new life now that he'd made a significant career decision. "We can celebrate your future as an oil executive."

It sounded a world away from ranch foreman, a job that had defined the Xander she knew.

Still, she couldn't deny that he seemed happier. Freer. As if he'd made peace with his past and was ready to move on. Frankie felt glad if she'd played a small role in helping him get there. Glad for his sake, anyway.

For her own, she was already feeling him pulling away to embrace the life he was meant to lead. One that didn't include an orphaned, runaway cowgirl with big dreams and an uncertain future.

Frankie had barely made it to the mall before closing after her volunteer shift at the animal shelter, but she'd been determined to buy an outfit worthy of another glitzy Texas Cattleman's Club function.

But the rush to shop—and the sting of parting with the extra cash for an outfit— paid off when she walked into the fancy Haciendas meeting space the next day in her sleek white sheath dress and matching short-sleeved jacket. While she knew without question that Annabel would have helped her in the wardrobe department, it seemed good to have chosen her own clothes. Today, she wasn't the Cinderella beauty she'd been at the gala—a look that wasn't really *her*. In today's smart peep-toe pumps and fitted dress, she felt like the business professional she one day hoped to be.

She'd put her hair in a low ponytail, neat and simple. With a gold bangle on her wrist, she was done accessorizing. And as she glanced around at the other women who attended the meeting and cocktail hour that followed it, Frankie felt she'd done a good job of choosing her outfit. Angela Perry was pretty and understated in a dark-cherry-colored skirt with a lightweight black blouse that had sheer sleeves. Her twin, Melinda, wore a more sophisticated suit that could have come straight off a Paris runway, but it wasn't anything Frankie would have been comfortable wearing.

"You look incredible," Xander whispered in her ear as the formal meeting broke up and the social networking began.

The Haciendas historic property was made up of four buildings just outside downtown.

The largest of them served as today's venue. The high cathedral ceilings were made of rich, dark wood, the oiled bronze fans spinning silently overhead. Whitewashed stucco walls and dark wood floors gave the place a Spanish feel echoed in the simple, heavy furnishings. Red hibiscus arrangements were the only pops of color.

"Thank you," Frankie murmured as she helped herself to a glass of seltzer water from a passing waiter while the staff steered the guests onto a large patio addition. Bamboo plants and potted palms lined the walls. "It's unlike me to splurge on clothes, but if this is my last chance to spend time with the Texas Cattleman's Club for a while—"

"Why would it be the last chance?" Xander asked, his hand briefly touching the small of her back.

He stopped off to the side of the room while the rest of the Texas Cattleman's Club organizing members moved onto the patio that extended outdoors. A bar was set up on the far end of an outdoor garden, and a lone classical guitar player strummed a tune near a wall of live plants. The volume of the party turned up a notch, everyone relieved to have the business part of the day behind them.

Even Sterling Perry seemed content to stay on the opposite side of the room from his rival, Ryder Currin.

Frankie wished she could simply focus on the party and regretted her verbal misstep, since Xander hadn't officially told her that things were over between them. But she wanted to make things easier for him.

For both of them.

"I just mean—I know you're taking the job with Currin Oil, so we won't be seeing each other as much."

His head tipped to one side as he studied her. "Why would you think that?"

She was saved from answering the question when Xander's father, Ryder, appeared over Xander's shoulder.

"Hello, Frankie. I'm sorry to interrupt,

but, Xander, I wonder if you would consider keeping an eye on things for a few minutes while I step out to speak to Angela?" Ryder glanced over his shoulder toward where Sterling held court near the bar. "We don't need a repeat of what happened at the Flood Relief Gala."

"Of course." Xander nodded, but he kept his focus on Frankie.

Her belly knotted from nerves. She really didn't want to upset Xander, especially when she'd hoped to use the meet and greet as a chance to network.

"You should introduce Frankie around." Ryder smiled down at her, his blue eyes so like his son's. "I'm sure she'd like the chance to speak to Zane Daughtry. His son is a veterinarian in Galveston, you know."

"I'll do that," Xander assured him, his hand curving possessively around her hip as he shifted closer. "Thanks, Dad."

When Ryder moved away, Frankie peered around the room. "Which one is Zane Daughtry?" she asked, hoping to distract Xander from the conversation they'd been having.

But before Xander could answer, an auburn-haired beauty stopped in front of them, gasping audibly as her eyes met Frankie's.

Noticing the other woman, Xander pasted on his social smile. He greeted the newcomer kindly enough, but his cadence sounded stilted as he spoke. "Good to see you, Abby." He followed the woman's gaze to Frankie, clearly recognizing that Abby stared at her openly. "Have you met Frankie Walsh? Frankie, meet Abigail Langley."

Frankie had the strangest sensation looking at the woman. Abby Langley was probably in her mid- to late-thirties, with long red waves. But the most striking thing about her was that she gaped at Frankie as if she'd seen a ghost.

"How do you do, Ms. Langley?" Frankie said politely, offering her hand.

"Pardon me for staring." The woman's voice was whisper thin before she blinked and continued, louder this time. "That mark on your neck, my dear. I'd swear it's the Langley birthmark."

The floor felt like it opened up beneath Frankie as she absorbed those words. Her hand went to her neck.

"My birthmark?" she repeated, not understanding.

"Most of the women in my family are born with it," Abigail informed her. "And you'd be just the right age. How old are you?"

"I'm sorry. I'm confused." She gripped Xander's free hand, needing it to ward off the faintness she felt as a buzzing started in her ears.

Xander intervened, his tone concerned. "Abby, what are you talking about?"

"Your eyes are just the right shade of green." Abigail still stared at Frankie, to the point their conversation was attracting attention from the rest of the party. "My cousin, Josie Langley, lost her little girl twenty-three years ago in a flood like the one that rocked Houston this spring. And I can't help but notice you bear more than a passing resemblance to Josie. That's why I gasped when I saw you."

Abby Langley pulled her phone from her leather clutch and flipped through screens while Frankie tried to get her head around what she was suggesting.

The room started to spin. The math added up, since Frankie was indeed twenty-five years old. And her parents had claimed to have found her when she was two.

"You think that I could be—"

Abby flipped her phone around to show Frankie a photo of an attractive woman with dark hair and green eyes. The expression on the brunette's face was familiar because it was the same one Frankie glimpsed in the mirror every day.

The woman in the photograph bore her an uncanny resemblance. An older version of Frankie herself.

"Even without the birthmark, I would have been stunned at your resemblance," Abby said, her hand trembling as she shared the picture. "But considering that distinctive crescent moon on your neck, my dear, I'd say there's an excellent chance that you're the lost Langley heiress."

Ten

An hour later, Xander sat beside Frankie in one of the historic inn's private rooms close to the Texas Cattleman's Club meet and greet. He hadn't known where else to go with her to have an uninterrupted conversation, so he'd flagged down one of the event organizers and requested accommodations.

Frankie had been so pale after the intense encounter with Abigail Langley that he'd been worried about her. Now, they sat in a glassed-in sunroom off the back of a secluded hacienda on the ground floor. They could look out over the meet and greet spilling out onto the inn's private grounds in the larger hacienda nearby, but he didn't think anyone could see into their suite with the way the windows were tinted.

He'd ordered a tray of food from catering, but so far Frankie hadn't shown any interest in the five-star offerings. She sat on a leather upholstered chair at a heavy hardwood table, her fingers clamped around a mug of tea that she'd accepted from him even though she hadn't taken a single sip. She stared out at the cocktail party going on without them, but her green eyes were unfocused.

"Should we call someone? Your parents, perhaps?" he suggested gently, not wanting to upset her. "If you shared what Abigail told you, maybe they could offer more answers for you. One way or another."

He wasn't sure what he believed about Abby's shocking revelation. While he couldn't deny Frankie bore a resemblance to the Langley relative whose picture he saw on the phone, he also didn't want to get her hopes up. What if Abby's insistence that Frankie was heir to the Langley fortune was born out of the woman's own desire for family? It sounded far-fetched to find a long-lost relative in a crowded cocktail party.

After her pronouncement, Abigail had been ready to arrange for Frankie to have DNA testing, but Xander had asked for some time to digest the news since he'd seen how upset Frankie was. He'd then promptly spirited her away. He would have left the party altogether but that would have necessitated walking through the crowd. The deserted side room offered a speedier, more private respite.

"Why would my adoptive parents start telling me the truth now?" She lifted the mug toward her lips and then hesitated, setting it back on the table, her hands trembling, her voice tight, angry. "I asked them for answers my whole life, and all that ever accomplished was a greater commitment to keeping me isolated from the rest of the world."

Isolated because they were protective? Or

because they'd kidnapped her? She had to be wondering the same thing.

"But if they knew about this—about Abby Langley's insistence you're a relative—maybe they could at least give you enough details to explain why that couldn't be true."

If they weren't kidnappers. Although there were other options, like a sketchy adoption with someone else at fault.

"You don't think it's true?" She peered across the table at him where he sat diagonally from her. Her gaze was focused now. Intent. "That I'm this long-lost heiress?"

A candle in the table's centerpiece flickered in the breeze from an overhead fan, the surrounding fresh sunflower blooms rustling slightly.

"That's not what I'm saying. I just meant that your parents might share enough facts to quickly disprove it, and save you from the angst of waiting for DNA test results."

He couldn't help but feel protective of her. Her pain reached out to him, drawing him in and making him hurt for her.

"Or they could hedge, the way they always have, and make me all the more resentful that I lost out on a normal childhood because they were continually worried someone would show up with a better claim to me." She set aside the tea and stood, pacing over to the wall of windows looking out on the cocktail party.

The blue glow of the lighted swimming pool illuminated the garden as the sun set, the landscape spotlights flickering on automatically.

Not sure how to comfort her when he had the same concerns, Xander followed her to stare out over the festivities. He slid an arm around her waist, drawing her against him. She fit there perfectly, her head tucked under his chin. He tipped his cheek against the silky strands of her hair.

"No one can claim you now, though, Frankie," he reassured her. "You are your own woman. Everything you've achieved, you've accomplished on your own. And that's a lot to be proud of."

"But how much easier might it have been with the help of a family?" She edged back a step to look at him. "I've tried to cram a lifetime worth of experiences in the last seven years since I left home, desperate to make up for the way I couldn't do anything as a kid. The ranch work, bronc riding, straight As in school, volunteering my free time at the shelter—I was starving for a taste of the world."

Had their affair been another facet of her attempt to taste the world? The realization stung. He hadn't guessed that about her, although perhaps he should have made the connection. He admired how high-achieving she was, but had her need for experiences come at a price? To both of them?

"No one can take away what you've accomplished," he insisted, wondering if she understood how impressive it was to be on the verge of veterinary school when she'd done it all on her own. "No one can say you got where you are because of your family."

"Maybe I wouldn't have minded some

help." Folding her arms, she glared out at the party continuing without them. "The Perrys and the Currins might vie for an advantage over each other, but they're both very sure of their place in the world. Just the name— either name—gives you power."

"You want it to be true." He hadn't been sure of that until now, hearing the edge in her voice. "You *want* to be the Langley heiress, don't you?"

She turned back to him. This time, the pain in her green eyes was startlingly clear.

"Who in their right mind would choose to be an orphan over a woman with family and connections? A family whose powerful name could have given me the kinds of advantages you've had?"

Intellectually, he could see her point. Of course he could.

That didn't mean he was as ready to embrace her future as a Langley. Everything between them would change. Both of their families would take an interest in their relationship. The Langleys and the Currins—

two well-known Texas families—would each have a stake in their dating lives. There would be more pressure. More scrutiny.

More of the suffocating atmosphere that had made Rena want to escape from their engagement.

Then again, would a Langley heiress even want to date the Currin who'd been working as a ranch foreman? He hadn't stepped into the Currin Oil CEO role yet. Things were already shifting between them faster than he could keep up.

"My family may have given me advantages," he acknowledged carefully, returning to the catering tray left on the sideboard to escape the naked anguish in her expression. Or was it so that she didn't see his? He wanted to pour himself a drink, but there was nothing but sparkling water and an unopened bottle of champagne on the tray. And this hardly felt like a celebration. He took a deep breath before continuing, "But like you, I've worked hard to get where I am. And you can't deny that you've enjoyed the privileges that come with the Currin name. The access to the Texas Cattleman's Club, for example. The networking for your future."

Giving up on the drink he wanted, Xander pivoted back toward Frankie. She was staring at him as though she was seeing him for the first time, her expression puzzled.

"I have appreciated that, Xander." Her reasonable tone didn't do anything to soothe his sense of things falling apart.

He could feel the thin foundation of their affair crumbling beneath his feet.

"But you won't need my help any longer once you're a Langley, will you?" he pressed, seeing the truth of what being an heiress meant for her. "With your inheritance, you certainly won't need to work on the ranch. You'll have all the backing you'd need for membership in the Texas Cattleman's Club. Hell, Abby's a past president of the Royal branch, so you're in good hands there. She's surely better connected than I am."

He wanted to stop the flow of words, to shut down the certainty that this was the end of them. He knew he was being unfair to her. They didn't even know for sure that she was a Langley. But the thought of losing her like this was tearing him apart. More than it should. And that had him itching to run, far and fast.

"I didn't enter this relationship for the help," she shot back with a fierceness in her tone, revealing that he'd touched a nerve. "If you'll recall, I was ready to buy my own ticket to the gala."

Damn it.

This was not the conversation he should be having with her right now. Especially here, with partyers only a stone's throw away. But right or wrong, they were stuck with this conversation. Consequences be what they may.

"By risking your neck," he reminded her wryly. "I remember. You were prepared to succeed without me then. But now we've shared something, even if it was a fling. I think you owe me at least a goodbye if you're intending to walk away."

"I never said I wanted to end…this." She

hugged herself tighter, more beautiful in her simple white dress than any of the socialites draped in jewels and designer outfits mingling at the party that played out through the glass behind her.

"You didn't have to." His chest ached to look at her, so delicate and strong at the same time. "You've been preparing for the end of this affair ever since the first night we spent together. You left that time, Frankie. Not me." The sense of loss closed over him like a dark cloud. Smothering him. He needed to get away from here.

"That's not fair," she told him softly, her green eyes wounded, yet she didn't draw near him.

None of it was fair. That didn't make the hurt any less real.

He backed up a step to retrieve his truck keys from the table. "I'm going to get some fresh air. The room is all yours for the night if you want it."

"I don't." She lobbed the retort his way as he headed for the door.

Of course she didn't want the room. He shouldn't be surprised. Xander didn't have one damned thing left to offer her anymore.

Frankie stared out the sunroom windows of the private hacienda, watching the beautiful party going on without her or Xander.

The sun had fully set since he stormed out of the private lodging, the quiet descending on her like a shroud after their heated exchange. It hadn't been an argument, really. But the darker emotions it had churned in her were volatile enough.

And she knew it had done the same for him. She'd heard it clearly enough in his voice right before he'd walked away.

Not in a million years would she have guessed she could wield the power to hurt Xander Currin, a man she'd viewed as invincible to softer emotions, judging by the revolving door of women he'd dated. But that hadn't been fair of her. She'd assumed that he lacked deeper feelings, when he'd simply locked them away as effectively as she had.

He had been protecting himself after the loss of his fiancée. She'd been protecting herself against the abandonment that had been burned into her nature at a young age. Maybe she should have recognized his kindred spirit, but she'd been so busy worrying about the risk to her own heart she hadn't given enough thought to his.

Now Frankie took in the lush garden setting just outside the window, seeing it without being a part of it. What a perfect metaphor for her whole life. Always on the outside looking in. She'd never had a deep sense of family from the couple who'd raised her. Never had a sense of belonging until she'd come to Currin Ranch, where her "family" was made up of grizzled wranglers and herdsmen. Even there, she'd had different dreams than them, wanting to work with the animals more than the people.

The shock of Abigail Langley's revelation was making her feel even more untethered than usual. Every abandoned child dreamed of unlikely scenarios like this one—a stranger sees beyond the surface to the person she was born to be. But Frankie had outgrown dreams like that long ago, so she wasn't going to get suckered into some fanciful vision of her future.

An heiress.

She couldn't even imagine how radically that would change her life. She wouldn't have to scrimp every cent for veterinary school and for a place of her own one day. Even more importantly, she would be able to afford to focus all her time on her studies instead of working to support herself. That would be…too incredible.

Aside from the obvious benefits of money, Frankie would belong. Xander had a point about not needing him—she would have her own place in the Texas Cattleman's Club. A privileged family who would help her secure that spot.

Yet just because she didn't need Xander didn't mean she wouldn't want him. She feared she would always want him, whether he wanted her or not.

She didn't know how much time she passed
staring out at the party, picking through her
feelings, but a swish of blond hair outside
drew her attention to where Angela Perry
and her father were having an intense private conversation beneath a sprawling old
live oak tree, hidden from view of the rest
of the party. Father and daughter. Family.

As much as Sterling seemed overbearing
and far too intrusive in his daughter's life, at
least Angela had the certainty that she was
deeply loved. The longing for family inten-
sified the ache in Frankie's heart.

Did she want to rejoin the glittering party
on the other side of the windows? This time,
she would be all alone. No Xander to smooth
her way or make introductions.

Should she hold her head up high and force
herself into the future? Go back to the party
and tell Abigail Langley she'd take the DNA
test, even if she didn't understand how she
could possibly be a Langley?

It would be easier to hide in the private
room Xander had reserved for them, nursing

the ache in her chest that burned ever since his parting words. But that had never been in her nature. Xander had been correct about that much. Even if it meant risking her neck, she would forge ahead.

In this case, maybe what she really needed to risk was the piece of her she'd guarded so carefully. The heart that she'd wanted to keep safe from Xander at all costs.

But first, she needed to get some answers about who she was, even if meant going back to Laredo and facing the home she'd run from the moment she'd turned eighteen.

Angela Perry hadn't wanted to confront her father here—at the cocktail reception following the Texas Cattleman's Club planning meeting. But her dad had a way of forcing his own agenda, demanding to speak with her privately unless she wanted another very public showdown.

As if *she'd* been the one to initiate their argument at the Flood Relief Gala.

"I thought I made myself very clear regarding that bastard Ryder Currin," her father fumed, his eyes narrowing. His Stetson and boots were both brand-new, and diamond cufflinks in the shape of horseshoes glittered at his wrists.

Her father was a very different man from Ryder.

Angela clutched her purse tighter, mindful of eyes all around them, even if they were tucked behind the trunk of an old live oak. The landscape lighting kept the garden area in a golden glow as the temperature dropped enough for more people to venture outside in the June heat. Strategically placed outdoor fans kept air circulating.

"You made it clear you'd rather be unreasonable than listen to what I have to say." Angela's eyes found Ryder on the other side of the party, his dark Stetson a perfect complement to his jeans and jacket.

His ease in his own skin had always attracted her. He'd never needed anything flashy for himself, and she liked that about him. She wasn't going to pretend otherwise for her father's sake.

"Are you aware of the rumors?" Sterling demanded, the cords in his neck standing out visibly as his anger ratcheted up.

"I am," she told him defiantly, shifting position on her heels so they didn't sink into the soft earth. "I know about the alleged affair with Mom, and I don't believe it for a minute. I know you don't, either, or you would have settled that with Mom long ago."

Sterling wasn't the kind of man who would take that offense lying down. Angela's mother must have been able to prove her innocence. Or else Sterling had never had a shred of evidence to begin with. Angela wasn't going to let a whisper campaign prevent her from finding happiness with Ryder.

"Ryder Currin has tried to undermine me my whole life." He pointed at her with the tip of his longneck bottle. "Do you really think you mean anything more to him than as a tool to weaken Perry Holdings?"

Angela tried to ignore the hurt that came

with the words—the implication that she meant nothing to Ryder.

"I believe I have more appeal than that, Dad. And I also believe I'm too important to Perry Holdings for you to dismiss me just because you don't want me to have a relationship with Ryder. My personal life is my business. Not yours."

Her father looked ready to explode with anger. Angela debated walking away before he could respond, but she knew that would only delay the inevitable confrontation. Besides, there were two men in poorly fitting suits headed their way. Something about them appeared off, alerting her they didn't belong here. One of them was gray-haired and grizzled. The other tall, thin, with a clean-shaven face that made him look like he was barely out of college.

A handful of party guests turned to watch their progress through the crowd toward Angela and her father. As they neared, one of them pulled out a badge.

The police.

"Dad," she said, keeping her voice low. "We have company." Then, to the closest police officer, she asked, "What's going on?"

Sterling turned to see the men, then stepped closer to Angela. "I'm sure it's just about the body at the TCC renovation site," he reassured her.

A bad feeling made her stomach sink. The officers didn't look friendly. And their attention was fixed firmly on her father.

"Sterling Perry?" the gray-haired shorter of the pair asked, shoving his badge back inside his jacket pocket.

"Yes," her father answered.

A glint of metal distracted her and she realized in slow-motion horror that the younger officer withdrew a pair of handcuffs.

"Sterling Perry, you're under arrest for conspiracy to commit fraud. You have the right to remain silent—"

The rest of the words were lost on Angela in her shock. Stunned, she struggled to take in the pandemonium around her. Her father began shouting that he was innocent even as the handcuffs went around his wrists. Angela's knees turned to liquid under her. Stumbling forward, she felt blindsided as the arresting officer continued to read a laundry list of charges that made it sound like her father had masterminded a Ponzi-style scheme.

What the hell? She hadn't even known he was under criminal investigation. All her anger at him from earlier in the evening evaporated as she saw him in handcuffs. He was her father and this couldn't be true.

Beside her, her twin sister, Melinda, suddenly appeared, linking hands with her and squeezing so tightly her fingers went numb.

"Why is this happening?" She glanced over at Melinda. Her twin was usually so unflappable, but her viselike grip relayed her own disconcerted feelings.

"I don't know, but I'm afraid it's going to get worse before it gets better," she said softly, careful not to be overheard. "Once investors get wind of this, they will start to panic, wanting to sell their shares."

Melinda didn't have to spell out what that meant. Widespread fear for their finances would result in too many shareholders trying to cash in at once. Which meant a whole lot of good people could go broke, even if her father wasn't guilty.

I staked out an excellent view of Sterling Perry's dramatic exit. Of course, it was easy to put myself in a good position since I may have leaked a few things to the police. When Ryder and Angela didn't have quite the splashy public breakup I was hoping for, I will admit I began getting antsy for things to start happening.

Having Sterling behind bars will do wonders for my plan. Public opinion will shift quickly now. People who held Sterling in such high regard are sure to turn on him overnight. What perfect punishment for him, considering how quickly my life went up in flames because of Sterling Perry and Ryder Currin.

I remember all too well how that felt. How it still feels. My lost family. My lost wealth and privilege. Sure, I'd salvaged the pretense of reasonable success, but it was nothing compared to my old life.

Seeing Angela and Melinda now, holding hands while they worry about their precious father, reminds me how I have no children in my life to worry about me. I hate that Sterling has that kind of support. Even as I celebrate seeing him taken away by the police, I regret that I can't yank everything out from under him all at once.

Patience.

Strolling out of the gardens, I step inside the main building into the cool air-conditioning. It's better not to get overheated or overzealous about the revenge scheme. One thing at a time, and I need to be satisfied with the progress I make each day toward my revenge. Because rushing the agenda only adds a risk to getting caught.

And I refuse to let that happen.

* * *

From the opposite side of the garden, Xander saw Sterling being taken away in handcuffs.

He'd lingered outside the suite he'd obtained for Frankie, knowing he should figure out a way through their problems. Yet before he could come up with the right words to say to her that might smooth things over, the police had arrived to cart Sterling off the property. An absolute disaster of an evening from start to finish.

Even now from his vantage point near the outdoor bar, Xander could see Frankie silhouetted in the sunroom window by the candlelight behind her, the white dress making her easier to see. Then again, his eyes would be drawn to her anywhere, anytime.

His lungs constricted around a breath while the Texas Cattleman's Club party dissolved into tense conversations, panicked phone calls and a sea of gossip. The anxiety of seeing Sterling being taken away was affecting everyone—friend and foe alike.

Xander knew he should check in with his father, who might have his hands full comforting Angela in the aftermath of this latest adversity. But he couldn't quite tear his gaze from Frankie when he knew she must be in shock over Abigail Langley's revelations.

Whether or not she was the missing heiress, Frankie deserved his support. Yet he couldn't forget how completely she'd withdrawn from him afterward. Just like Rena had.

It would haunt him forever that he hadn't seen the signs of his fiancée's unhappiness before her untimely death. He'd never had the chance to find out why she'd broken things off so suddenly, and he had been completely unaware that she'd wanted to end it. Now, in the first significant relationship he'd had since then—the first relationship that really meant something to him—he'd missed the bigger picture once again.

Wrestling with his conscience about walking away, he knew he needed to talk to Frankie. When his cell phone vibrated in his jacket pocket, he felt a moment's hope that she'd reached out to him. Checking the screen, however, he saw a text from his father.

We need to meet. Now.

Damn it. The whole Texas Cattleman's Club community would feel the reverberations of Sterling's arrest. Xander understood he needed to help his father put out fires.

Maybe it was best that he and Frankie take time to think through things after their exchange anyhow. For tempers to calm. He'd talk to her once cooler heads prevailed.

And even as he told himself that, Xander suspected he was just avoiding the truth of what his gut was telling him—that he'd already fallen in love with Frankie and he was scared as hell she would never love him back.

Eleven

Four days after the party, Xander still hadn't seen Frankie. He'd left her a message that he hoped to see her, but didn't want to pressure her. Especially since he'd been the one to walk out on a night that must have been devastating for her.

He regretted that deeply, even as he knew he would while it was all unfolding. But he hadn't been ready for Abby Langley's surprise announcement, let alone what it meant for his future with Frankie.

If there was such a thing. He might have

destroyed any chance he had for a future with her by not putting her first when she needed him most.

Giving in and rapping on the door to her cabin, he figured she must be avoiding him. He'd been working almost nonstop since the Texas Cattleman's Club planning meeting, the fallout from Sterling's arrest spilling over into the new Houston branch as members questioned whether Sterling belonged in the club.

That work had taken up much of Ryder's time, giving Xander more work with Currin Oil. His father was thrilled to have him in the office, and Xander was glad he was finally stepping into the role he'd always planned to have with the company. Especially since he knew his second-in-command on the ranch would finally have a chance to test out the foreman role. But it meant he hadn't been on the ranch to see Frankie.

"Frankie," he called as he knocked a second time.

The only sound he heard in response was

a raven cawing at him from her porch rail. Overhead, the late-afternoon sun beat down with an oppressive heat.

"She's out of town, boss," a man's voice called to him from the grassy ranch road.

Xander turned to see Reggie Malloy, the longtime member of the Currin Ranch team who'd been there the night of the rodeo when Xander had talked Frankie out of competing.

"Out of town?" Xander stepped off the small porch of the cabin, heading down the path toward the dirt road where Reggie sat on a spotted Appaloosa.

"She asked Len for a couple of personal days. Said something about going to see her folks in Laredo, I heard." Reggie tipped his hat up, mopping his forehead with the sleeve of his work shirt.

No surprise that Reggie knew about the trip, since word spread fast in a small community like theirs. Len, Xander's second-in-command, oversaw more of the personnel concerns. What bugged Xander was that he hadn't heard a thing about it. Why would she risk a confrontation with her parents by herself? Damn it, he knew he should have checked on her sooner. In giving her time to cool off, had he pushed her away completely?

He hated the idea that she would see her parents alone after all this time.

But he'd lost the right to weigh in on those decisions when he'd walked away from her after the meet and greet. The need to be with her, to lend whatever support he could, was so strong he wanted to get in his truck now and start driving. Lost in his own thoughts, he was surprised when Reggie spoke up again.

"Do you think it's true she's going to turn out to be the lost Langley heiress?" The saddle creaked under Reggie as he shifted his weight. "We heard what happened at the Texas Cattleman's Club meeting—about Abigail Langley recognizing that birthmark."

"I'm not sure what to believe." Xander's gut told him it was probably true; however, he didn't want to speculate about her when she wasn't involved in the conversation.

He knew she'd probably already made her decision about whether or not to submit a DNA test, but he hoped to at least speak to her before she got the results back, if that was the route she'd chosen. He needed to assure her it didn't matter to him what the results said—that he wanted her in his life no matter what.

Reggie grinned from atop the Appaloosa. "Hard to imagine that one of the toughest hands on the payroll might turn out to be as good as Texas royalty. But we told her she's got a place with us forever either way."

Clicking softly to his horse, the herd driver set the Appaloosa in motion, leaving Xander there alone with his thoughts.

It didn't speak well of him that the staff of Currin Ranch all knew exactly what to say to Frankie when she'd been confronted with a dramatic revelation about her birth, whereas Xander had put his foot in his mouth and left her to face the consequences alone.

But he intended to fix that. Right now.

* * *

Tossing her rubber apron in a bin outside the back door of a local veterinary practice, Frankie went inside to scrub off the day of volunteer work in the field. She'd put in almost eight hours with Doc Macallan in the mobile veterinary van, visiting sick calves, a wounded horse and one very unhappy pig with an infected hoof. The vet lived on the property, in a farmhouse nearby, and had already retreated to his home for the evening, hoping to leave for a fishing trip as soon as he cleaned up.

She was on her second round of antibacterial soap up to her elbows when her phone chimed with a text message. She glanced over at the counter above the sink, where she could see the sender's name.

Xander.

Her chest ached and she found her eyes reading the text before she could debate the wisdom of it.

Flying to Laredo ASAP. Please wait to speak
to your parents until I can be there.

Surprised, she dried her hands quickly.

The parting with Xander might have hurt,
but that didn't mean she wanted him to waste
a flight. Two of the other clinic staffers had
left for the day, leaving her alone at the practice with the vet's niece, who was playing
with a kitten one of their clients had found
abandoned by the highway and decided to
keep.

Just like me, Frankie thought wryly. She'd
been adopted into a strange home, too. Except the family who'd found her hadn't
wanted to look too closely at the truth of
where she'd come from. They'd hidden her
away from the world on purpose, to prevent
her real family from finding her.

And now she had the DNA test results
back that proved in no uncertain terms she
was a Langley. The confidential letter from
the laboratory had been waiting for her when
she'd returned from Laredo. Abigail Langley

had paid extra to rush the results, but she'd been kind enough to have the correspondence shipped solely to Frankie so she could have time to think about how she wanted to handle the information.

She still hadn't decided.

Settling into one of the break room chairs near the coffeepot, Frankie typed a response to Xander while the weariness of the day caught up with her. Ranch hand work took a physical toll, but her efforts with the animals took an emotional one. Even the victories in the field could be tiring, as frantic owners worried about their pets and distressed animals needed soothing. As she let the exhaustion roll over her, she tried to contain the spark of hopefulness she felt at hearing from Xander.

Not in Laredo anymore. Finishing shift at Macallan Clinic.

She guessed he must have learned her whereabouts from one of the guys at Currin

Ranch, since the other ranch hands were the only people who'd known she'd wanted to go home this week. She hadn't wanted to hear the DNA test results until she'd given her parents an opportunity to tell her the truth.

Not that she'd had any luck.

The next text was almost immediate.

Please don't leave. I'd like to speak to you.

To call it quits for good? To tell her he'd had time to think it over and he was more certain than ever that they weren't a good match? Those were her fears. But her hopes were quite different. She'd missed him these last several days while she'd been finding the courage to speak to him.

Okay.

She hit Send on the message, unable to say more than that when her feelings were in knots. She'd been so busy indulging her crush on Xander—so determined to squeeze all the pleasure out of a relationship with him—that she'd missed the chance to really get to know him.

To understand him.

To find common ground.

So now that their relationship was falling apart, she didn't have a clear idea how to talk to him about the things that mattered. About those hopes and fears of hers.

She guessed he had plenty of his own, too. Maybe she'd be able to see them now that she'd stopped viewing him as an unattainable hottie and started looking at him as a man.

A smart, caring, generous man, who'd extended himself to help her even when she hadn't been able to give him anything in return. No matter what else came of their relationship, she owed him a debt of gratitude for the connections she'd made within the Texas Cattleman's Club. The access to more potential references for veterinary school. The possibility of new volunteering opportunities that would give her the hours she needed to work with animals.

But what she still craved was *him*.

The anguish in her heart this week hadn't really been rooted in the DNA test results or her choices about her future with her family or career. All the pain had been over losing Xander. She had the courage to face a lot of challenges, it seemed, but the thought of life without Xander had the power to bring her to her knees.

When the knock sounded on the back door of the clinic, Frankie felt an answering thump of her heartbeat. Spearing to her feet, she hurried out of the break room to open the door.

Xander stood on the top step, wearing jeans and a gray jacket, his dark Stetson shielding his face from the late-afternoon sun. The frisson of awareness that jolted her was familiar by now, but it amazed her that it never seemed to fade. She realized that she'd been kidding herself to think an affair might quench her thirst for this man. The more time she spent with him, the more she wanted him.

The deeper she fell in love with him.

She understood that now.

Behind him, the vet's rural practice had an almost-empty parking area except for his truck and the vet's mobile treatment van. Nearby pens held some of the large animals that were recovering from surgery. A couple of older horses munched their hay while a solitary ostrich squawked unhappily in an enclosure of her own.

"Hi." Frankie stood on the threshold, her gaze greedily soaking Xander in after the days spent apart. Longing pierced her heart. "You got here fast."

She wondered what he was thinking behind those very blue eyes. She'd always known that he wouldn't stay in her life, but she hadn't recognized how much it would devastate her when he left. Thinking about the mystery of her birth these last few days had been—for once in her life—a welcome distraction from thinking about Xander.

From wishing she knew how to fix things between them.

"I was halfway to the private airstrip to take a flight to Laredo," he admitted. He turned to look out over the vet's small farm. "Is there anywhere we can speak privately?"

"Sure." She waved goodbye to the vet's niece before she closed and locked the door behind them, nervous and agitated. Scared, even, that she'd screwed things up irreparably. "There's a spot back here if you don't mind walking for a few minutes."

It was still hot outside, but Xander had spent long hours on the ranch in the Texas summer. She led them past the hog pen and donkey barn where Doc Macallan kept his own collection of animals. A rural windmill turned overhead, aerating a pond kept stocked with fish.

A few moments later, Xander must have caught sight of their destination—a round tent permanently erected on a wooden platform among the pine trees. A small deck extended from the front entrance, where a pair of Adirondack chairs sat side by side.

"A yurt?" Xander glanced from the tent

to her. It was a fleeting moment of shared amusement that made her wonder if she'd ever feel this connection to any human being again.

The amusement vanished.

"The vet calls it his retreat space." She'd visited the spot to have her lunch sometimes when the weather was cooler. "He left town for a long weekend, though, so it's all ours."

Xander followed her up the narrow steps to the deck under the shade of dense pine trees. She took a seat in one of the Adirondack chairs and Xander lowered himself into the other. He sat forward, though, on the edge of the chair, looking at her intently. He removed his hat and slid it on the wood railing along one side of the deck.

"First of all, I'm sorry you made that trip back home by yourself." The sincerity in his voice was unmistakable, but then, he was a kind, thoughtful person. "How did it go?"

Birds argued in the trees overhead, shaking a few needles down onto the soft earth. And Frankie was only too glad to talk about something besides the ashes of their relationship.

She seized on the topic gladly.

"I didn't learn anything." She'd made the decision to go impulsively, not wanting to call ahead to alert them to her arrival. "At least, not about my past. When I arrived at the home where I grew up, someone else was living there. Turns out my parents put that place on the market two months after I left home."

It had hurt to know they'd pulled up stakes so quickly. Not that they could have gotten in touch with her to tell her anyhow, since she'd changed her number deliberately to give herself space from their controlling ways. But their quick departure had told her they hadn't been concerned about keeping the house in case she wanted to return one day.

"You didn't get to see them?"

"No." She'd felt foolish when she got there. "I couldn't decide if I was relieved or disappointed that I drove five hours for nothing. I'm still not sure how I feel about that, but the fact is, I have no idea where to find them."

"A private investigator could track them quickly enough," he volunteered, shrugging out of the suit jacket and laying it over the arm of the chair.

She followed his movements, watching the play of muscle through the white cotton shirt. Wishing she still had the right to take shelter in his strong arms. But they'd lost themselves in physical attraction too many times, failing to build the deeper connection that might have helped them weather the last tumultuous week.

Had she lost that right forever?

Tension and wariness strung her nerves tight.

"I'm not sure that I want to contact them." She'd had a long time to think about it on the drive back to Houston and still wasn't sure of her next step where her adoptive parents were concerned. But she would phone the authorities and give a statement about what had happened so there was an official record of it. "I only made the trip because I thought it would be wise to give my parents an opportunity to come clean before I found out the results of the DNA test."

His mouth compressed into a flat line. Because he disagreed with her decision not to track her adoptive family? Or because he didn't think she should take the DNA test?

"Has Abigail Langley been in contact with you?" he asked, the question not revealing his thoughts.

"I spoke to her the night of the party—after Sterling's arrest—and agreed to go through with the test." Frankie had known she'd never get any sleep until she addressed the problem, and that meant finding out the truth one way or another. "I've asked her not to share the results with anyone for a few more days, even though she generously paid an exorbitant fee for rushed results."

Xander went still. Only the sound of a distant tractor and a few chirping birds broke the silence.

"You already know the results?" His dark eyebrows lifted.

"I do." She was still struggling to come to terms with the fact that she had parents out there she'd never met. A sister, too. Would her return to their family cause them upheaval or happiness? "You're the first person I've told. The first to know besides Abby and me that I'm a Langley."

She'd called Abigail after opening the letter to inform her, feeling that she deserved to know firsthand.

His hand clamped hers tightly, squeezing. "Frankie, I couldn't be happier for you."

The warmth of the words and the sentiment behind them were a welcome relief. She hadn't realized she'd been holding her breath until it huffed out in a sigh.

"Really? I wasn't sure how you'd react." Her gaze darted to where their hands remained clasped.

A friendly, empathetic gesture? Or could it mean more than that? Her nerves were stretched thin. The thought of losing him for good was killing her inside.

"I know I didn't express myself well the other night when we talked about it." He shook his head, regret tingeing his words. "What I was trying to say—while doing a poor job of it—was that you are an incredible person no matter your name. But knowing how difficult your childhood must have been, I'm happy that you will be surrounded by a very worthy family from now on. I've never met Abigail's cousin, but if Abby is any indication of the kind of family you come from, rest assured, you'll be very loved."

His words cheered her. Made her hopeful that he wouldn't turn his back on their friendship even if he wasn't ready to embrace a deeper relationship.

But she wanted it all. His heart. His love. Xander.

"Thank you." The restraint of not talking about them was starting to wear on her, her control fracturing as her voice caught. "That means a lot to me."

Nodding, she cleared her throat. Tried to get a hold of herself so she didn't fall apart in front of him.

Was she just delaying the inevitable?

"I'm surprised you aren't more eager to share the news with the world, though." He released his hold on her, making her very aware of the absence of his touch. "Is there any reason you don't want to tell people yet?"

"I'm still navigating what it means for me, so I'm not sure I'm ready to field the questions about what I'll do next." Tucking her feet under her seat, she looked out over the animal pens and picturesque old farm where she'd been volunteering for months, unwilling to think about what a life without Xander would look like. "Do I want to build a mixed practice like Doc Macallan? Specialize in large-animal medicine? Or forsake it all and go into a life of philanthropy now that I'm the heir to a fortune? What kind of obligation do I have to a family who mourned a lost child for twenty-three years?"

Of course, none of those worries mattered half as much as the one she didn't speak. The one she couldn't speak.

Sliding his chair closer, he draped an arm around her, squeezing her shoulder.

"Frankie, your first obligation is to yourself." He comforted her with his physical presence, and with his words even more so. "I know the Langley family, and they would be saddened to think they caused you a moment's unhappiness after all you've been through."

"I'm not unhappy." She didn't want to sound ungrateful. Part of her whole decision to wait with the news was so that she could avoid revealing the confusing mix of emotions. "The news is better than I ever could have hoped for. But after spending a lifetime feeling like I didn't fit in with my adoptive parents, I just don't want to be a disappointment to a new family."

"You could never be a disappointment."

His assurance warmed her, soothing the mix of fears that had been dogging her ever since she learned the good news. "More than anything, I wish I could have articulated that at the party the other night instead of letting my own concerns get in the way."

Bracing herself, she straightened, needing to be alert for this part of the conversation. She didn't want to misunderstand him or what was happening between them.

She also wanted to be very, very clear about what she hoped for. What she wanted.

"I think I was in a state of shock at the party," she admitted, remembering feeling distant from everything going on around her that night. "I didn't express myself well, either."

He let out a gusty sigh that she hoped was relief. If so, it could be a sign that he cared about saving this relationship, too.

"Do you mind if we have a rewind then? Go back and fix some of the things that didn't come out the right way?" He studied her, his arm sliding away again.

"I'd like that." She needed this second chance. She was determined not to waste it.

"When Rena broke off our engagement, I never found out why—not really. And I've avoided relationships since then because it made me wary that I couldn't see the signs when things were falling apart."

The simple truth made sense in retrospect. It certainly explained the endless parade of women before her. But at the time, it had felt like he'd been pulling away. As she stared down at her feet, trying to collect her thoughts, a chipmunk dived headfirst into a hole in the wooden decking.

"I didn't want to end things between us," she told Xander honestly, remembering the hurt and confusion of that conversation. "You were right that I've been bracing myself for the end, but only because I assumed you'd move on eventually and I didn't want you to take my heart with you when that happened."

This time, she gathered her courage and reached out to him. Taking his hand between both of hers, she held it tight, wishing she could impress upon him how much she still wanted things to work out.

"Xander," she continued, wanting to get it all out on the table before she lost her nerve. "All that time, I'd been thinking my heart was this tangible thing I could decide to give you or not. But I realized this week that I've had absolutely no control over it—no matter what I told myself. And as it turns out, I gave it to you that first night in the pool house."

The risk of revealing herself to him was the scariest thing she'd ever done. Bronc riding hadn't even been a close second. She held her breath, waiting for him to say something.

"You're telling me that I already have your heart?" His fingers flexed beneath hers, squeezing against her palm.

"I am." She nodded, nervous and anxious, but knowing that Xander deserved to hear those words from her.

Even if he didn't return the feeling.

"In that case…" He rose out of his chair and pulled her to her feet. Before she knew it, his arms were around her waist while they stood toe to toe. "I'm going to promise to take the best care of it." He kissed her cheek with a whisper-soft brush of his lips. "And I'm going to give you my heart in return, along with all my love."

Her lips parted in surprise, her heart pounding wildly.

But before she could ask for clarification on those points, his mouth was on hers, kissing her as if they had all the time in the world. As if this kiss was the most important thing that Xander Currin had to think about.

For a moment, she lost herself in that sweet dance of tongues and lips, the sensual draw pulling her in deeper. Making her hungry for more.

Then she recalled they'd gotten in trouble in the past from letting desire carry them away. Edging back, she tipped her face up to his.

"Can you repeat that last part, please?" Blinking away some of the dizzying chemistry, she focused on his eyes.

A warm, wicked laugh escaped him.

"Gladly." His words were a warm rumble against her skin, reverberating in his chest where the sound originated. "I said I love you, Frankie Walsh. Or Francesca Langley. No matter what name you go by, no matter your past. I love you when you're a muddy cowgirl, a studious vet school candidate or a breathtaking society beauty. Every facet of you mesmerizes me."

There was no answer for how deeply his words touched her. How very loved he made her feel by caring about those different aspects of her world.

So she kissed him again, with all the hope and longing in her soul. She kissed him until her knees were weak and she felt light-headed from the sweetness and sultriness of their bodies pressed together.

"Is it crazy to fall in love so fast?" she asked, even though she knew she'd been falling for him all year long. Her eyes had followed him everywhere, observing him every day, and she'd fantasized about him every night.

She might have started out with a crush, dreaming of an idealized version of Xander. But she knew him now. And loved him even more.

"Other people only dream of finding a love that feels like this," he said against the top of her head, kissing her hair. "So I'm not going to call it crazy. I'm going to say we're very, very lucky."

"Me, too." Her heart smiled, the knowledge that he was right filling her up inside. Making her happier than she'd ever been before. "Can we go home together now?"

She wanted this man all to herself for days on end.

"We can go anywhere you want," he promised, retrieving his Stetson and his jacket before he drew her forward into their future. "We've got a lot to talk about."

Her feet hurried on the path that led to his truck and, eventually, back to Currin Ranch.

"We do." She wrapped her arm around his

waist, tucking her hand into his back pocket. "But I think we should ease into all that conversation. Intersperse it with a lot of kissing…and things."

His hand squeezed her hip, a warm, delectable weight against her. "I can only drive so fast to get us home," he reminded her as they strode past the donkeys, pigs and goats.

"Right. We'd better stick to just talking until then." She tipped her head against his shoulder, full of hope and perfect contentment. "You can tell me what animals you like best since I'm envisioning a life surrounded by them."

She liked the vet's rural practice where he saw every kind of animal imaginable.

"As long as I get you in the bargain, it doesn't matter." Xander held open the passenger-side door for her and she climbed inside the big pickup truck.

"So you're saying you're open to an ostrich?" The exotic bird was still squawking loudly, driving the older horses to the far side of their pen to keep space between them.

"For you, I'd consider it." Xander leaned over in the truck to kiss her again, making her forget what they'd been talking about. "But maybe let's start with a dog and see what happens."

Buckling in, Frankie couldn't stop smiling. She had the man she loved by her side and a future sparkling with possibilities. It seemed romance was very much alive and well after all.

And she planned to do everything in her power to make sure it stayed that way.

* * * * *